DETARRU ISLAND

THE GATES OF HELL

MICKEY DEYMON

"To my sister Dorivee and my brother Jhovanny, who are both in heaven. This is for you guys"

CHAP†ER I

I'VE BEEN GOING THROUGH so many unexplainable, unimaginable and bizarre events these past few months that I think I've completely lost it.

When I first moved to New York City from California, I was in my new room unpacking my things. There were boxes stashed in every corner of my room and it was pretty difficult for anyone to get around much. I was about to place a pair of shoes in my closet when my father just barged in my room and sat on a chair near my bed without difficulty whatsoever.

Erick, I think we've found it!" he began shouting.

"What did you find?" I responded, not amused.

"Satu." he answered.

Suddenly an energy rush went through me and I walked across the room to where my dad was sitting, with no difficulties whatsoever either, and looked straight into his eyes.

"For real?" Where?"

"According to Craig, he should be somewhere in the jungles of Kilimanjaro, Africa," he finally answered.

Something didn't add up. Satu was a king that ruled over Detarru Island in 560 BC, an island isolated across the Atlantic Ocean. Not in Africa.

"Wait What? What's he doing all the way out there?"

"I have no idea," he answered.

"That's pretty weird."

"Indeed." His voice suddenly saddened. I knew something was bothering him.

"Okay, spill it," I said.

"What?" He turned to me not knowing what to say.

"I know you, Dad. You should be a lot more excited than this."

He looked down for a moment and then spoke.

"Well. I've spent a lot of money on this research and now that I'm this close to finding what I've been searching for so long, my budget is starting to run a little low," he said, disappointed. "I've asked The Glenwood Spring University of History and The New York National Museum to invest on this last expedition but none of the sponsors and executives have agreed to help. They said it has been a waste of time and that they're not going to spend any more money on my research."

My dad stood up and looked out my window. When he turned back to me, I noticed his weary eyes and shades of gray in his hair.

He looked tired.

So many years of hard work and dedication just to turn out to be a dead end. It must have been dreadful news to him. Ever since I was a little kid, he had taken me on all of his expeditions and I've been helping him with his research on Satu. I never thought I could learn so much about history from a simple artifact and to tell you the truth, I'm starting to love exploring new things every day. The thought of escaping your own reality and exploring new worlds is pretty remarkable to me and I enjoy every bit of it but it sounded like this was the end of our journey.

"What about Craig and Nathan? Can't they help with anything?" I said with a sense of hope.

Dr. Nathan Jeff is one of my father's closest protégés. When my father went on his first voyage to the Middle East together with Dr. Craig Halloway, they got lost in the Syrian Desert for about a week, with no food or water. That's when Nathan happened to be traveling on a journey and found them lying on the sand lifelessly under the burning, blistering sun. Ever since that day, my father, Craig and Nathan were the best of comrades. If there was anyone he could trust, it was certainly those two.

"I've already asked them," he replied.

"What did they say?" I asked impatiently.

"Well, Nathan said he'll get us there. I just don't know how he's planning to do that, without the money."

"What about Mom?" I added. "She can probably help us out"

My mother Clara Ross is an executive assistant at The Global Base Industry. A financial institution where they work out ways to stop the low and middle class struggles with debt.

Dad looked at me and started pacing back and forth as he registered that little piece of information in his brain. He then stopped and turned back to me.

"Erick! You're a genius! You think she'll say yes?"

"Who? Mom? Of course! Just leave it to me," I said, very confident and with heroic self-determination which was later crushed into bits by the very same mother I thought I could convince when she got home from work that night.

LATER THAT NIGHT

"What? Are you out of your mind? Absolutely not, child. Whose idea was this? Was it Jack's? Oh just wait till I see him." She took off her shoes and slammed her purse on the couch in the living room.

"But Mom? I really want to go."

"I almost lost you last time. Remember? You will not go on any of those hideous trips anymore."

"Mom?" I was six. And I didn't know how to swim then."

"Exactly! Your father should've been more careful with you, than with his stupid research."

"Mom?"

"I said no," she finished with an irritated gesture that would totally intimidate even the toughest WWE wrestler.

She sure hushed me. I was definitely not going to ask twice. I left the living room as soon as I had a chance. Deep inside I knew she was going to vent soon. Fortunately, not with me. The primary target was going to be my dad this time.

Poor guy, I thought.

If this was an opera play, this singer was just clearing her throat. Imagine what it would be like to hear her sing with such high-pitched vocals that would definitely make your ears bleed. Well, I didn't have to wait long for that answer. When I finally got to the end of the hallway and was heading up the stairs, I heard loud footsteps behind me. If I were an innocent bystander, I would've thought it was Big Foot, but this beast was definitely my mother, and she was heading straight to my father's sanctuary, his home office.

I ran to my room as quickly as possible, closed the door behind me and locked myself inside. I definitely didn't want to hear World War III in my house, but just in case things got out of hand, I leaned against the door just enough to hear what was going on out there.

Yea I know. I'm nosy.

Surprisingly, nothing happened. I started counting one through ten but there was still a deathless silence. This was something that threw me off completely, and I mean mentally. Growing up with my parents, I got to learn the rules when it had something to do with their deadly fights. Usually, my mom would make an exaggerated scene over anything, then ignore my father. If my father did it to her, she'd blow up like a loose cannon. Once the fight was over, they'd make up and forget about the whole thing but this time was different. For the first time in 16 years, I was wrong about this whole system.

Okay, maybe I exaggerated a little.

I opened the door just a little bit to peek outside and didn't see anything but a dark hallway. The only light I saw was coming from my room and my father's home office. His door was wide open and I was a little bit curious as to what was happening. I headed out to the hallway and walked towards the office and then I saw them.

For crying out loud. They were making out!!!

"What the?" I exclaimed confused.

I must have startled them. They both scattered across the room away from each other. Sort of like not wanting me to see the romantic scene.

Too late for that, I thought.

To my right, I noticed there was a rectangular-shaped gift and it looked like it had just been unwrapped. Mom turned around and faced me. She then took a few steps closer to me and I saw she had on an amazing silver necklace, which had a diamond-shaped crystal in the middle. It was the most beautiful thing I had ever seen and it sure looked great on her.

"I guess you're bling-blinging now... that's what's up," I said.

She kept throwing my father these flirtatious looks and I noted he was doing the same too. I felt like I was interrupting something.

If you know what I mean.

"It's beautiful isn't?" she asked. I nodded in agreement. "Your father remembered."

I turned to him to figure out what she talking about.

"Our 16th anniversary, Erick," he finally answered and winked at me.

That's all I needed.

I immediately got the message. I knew something was up and this was way too unusual to believe it was just an act of kindness. Dad went fishing and the fish just ate the bait. In this case, the diamond necklace was the bait and my mom just sunk her teeth into it.

"Wow, Dad! What a magnificent gift! Look at the diamond cut. Such perfection. Not to mention, it makes her look younger. Fine lady like her should be rocking them rocks," I said complimenting her.

"Oh, Jack, I feel terrible." She kept on, "I thought as usual you'd forget about our anniversary, so I never really bothered getting anything for you this year. I was selfish. Is there anything I could do to make it up to you?"

BINGO!

"Oh tell me, honey. Anything you want," she begged.

"Anything?" he asked with this wicked tone on his voice.

"Yes, anything."

He gave me a quick glance, as if letting me know he was victorious. Then said:

"Well, dear. I need your help."

Mom sat on a chair. "What's going on?"

"He faced the window that was located behind his desk. That's where he had been studying Detarru Island for years. The desk was filled with documents, maps scripts, and old books from the 14th century. On the right corner of the desk, almost on the edge, there was a picture frame of my grandparents and me, when I was a baby. My grandfather passed away two years ago from a car accident. Ever since then, my grandmother hadn't been doing very well emotionally and neither has my mother. Mom asked her to move in with us for a while, but she refused to leave Cali. I missed her, but especially granddad.

He used to take me out camping all the time in the summer, and I used to love fishing on his little boat.

My eyes got a little teary as memories came to my head.

"Clara? I don't want you to feel obligated to do this, but I would really appreciate it, with all my heart, if you could loan me some money from GBI?"

Mom stood up, a little bothered, and now looking down at him, replied, "Heaven sake, Jack! Is this about that...that... Satanini guy again?" she said, upset.

"The name is Satu," I corrected.

She turned and faced me as she folded her arms across her chest. I probably should've kept my mouth shut.

Note to self: Erick, keep your mouth shut when mom is upset.

Dad stood up and hugged her from behind. "You do not have

to do anything you do not wish to do," he finally said in this calm and passive way that would change your mind in a heartbeat, and to my surprise, it worked!

"Oh, alright then. How much money is it that you need?"

"About $100,000," he answered.

What?

That's a lot to ask for in such short notice. If my dad had a good chance of getting something out of this sugar mama, he totally blew it.

"Have you lost your mind?" she finally said.

"You know my crew has to get paid. Not to mention the expedition costs, and the excava—"

"Fine! But I'm coming too."

I looked at my dad, confused. She never went on any of our adventures, either because she was working or because she was simply not interested.

"Then, we'll have a great time together." My father smiled.

Oh brother.

THE NEXT DAY

Dad decided to have a meeting with Nathan and Craig in his office. They were talking about Satu and his whereabouts. While they discussed their flight plans, Mom was at GBI trying to negotiate a deal with the CEO to borrow the $100,000. So far, everyone was busy. As for me. I decided to walk around my new neighborhood and get some fresh air for a start. Making new friends this year was a priority. Besides, summer vacation was almost over in about a month and school was just around the corner.

Like literally!

I headed down Sunnyside Street, all the way to the next block up ahead, into an intersection and there it was.

Creston High School! The biggest high school I had ever seen. I walked to the school and as I crossed the street, I noticed a field. I couldn't tell if it was a soccer field or football from where I was standing. My hopes were on football, so I decided to find out. I walked around the school to see there was another brick building. It totally reminded me of the New York's Public Library. I figured it was a smaller version of the library in this school. I don't want to sound like a nerd but I kinda liked the idea of having a nice peaceful library I could study in and do homework. As I stood there, I heard voices. It was coming from the field. I kept walking and saw two guys batting some baseballs and another three catching them. I guess it was not a football field after all.

BUMMER.

I peered from behind the big fence and watched them play. Well, they were not really playing, but rather seemed like warming up. One of them was taller than the other and he was wearing a gray uniform, with black lettering and a black number 10. The other guy was wearing the same uniform but he was number 80. The tall guy, number 10, finally noticed me. He walked towards me and stood there, staring at me for a few seconds.

I felt a bit uncomfortable.

Number 80 seemed serious and had a game face on. To me, the guy looked ticked off. I couldn't really tell if he was pissed off at his team, or at the fact that I was just standing there like a nut sack. I didn't know what else to do, so I took a few steps backwards and backed away from the fence.

As I walked away, number 10 said, "Hey, you want to join us?"

I turned my head and gave him a sideways look.

"We want to start a game but we need more players. Do you play?" he asked.

I shrugged and said, "Sure."

He gestured to his team to regroup, then looked at me and pointed the way into the field. When everyone regrouped near number 10, I was introduced to the rest of the team.

Number 10 was Jimmy, African American, skinny tall guy with black hair and light brown eyes.

Number 3: Bruce, Caucasian, blonde, green eyes, dreadlocks, and a couple of inches taller than me.

Number 17: Luis, Latino, also taller than me. Brown hair and brown eyes. I overheard him speak Spanish and it sounded like a Dominican accent. Reason why I even know that is because I had a good friend in Cali who was also Dominican.

Number 80: Larry, Caucasian. He was average but a bit muscular too. He had brown hair and blue eyes and was a serious kind of guy. He sure looked pissed.

Number 22: Patrick, Asian American. When I first saw Patrick, he totally reminded me of Patrick Star from SpongeBob SquarePants. No Kidding! Only things missing were the triangular legs and arms. Okay, let me stop. He was a little overweight. Light skin, black hair and hazel almond eyes.

These guys seemed to be different ages. I couldn't really tell and I wasn't going to ask either.

Jimmy assigned me first base. I've always been good on first and second base. It was absolutely perfect!

Patrick was pitching and Larry had to take right field. I saw that Larry gave Jimmy a quick stern look. I think he wanted to pitch first. I was about to just let him have first base instead but he smiled at me, nodded, and ran off to right field. He was pretty much going to cover the whole outfield till it was his turn to pitch.

POOR GUY.

Jimmy was going to be first batter, Luis had second base, and Bruce had third. So far I liked these guys. They really worked as a team. I was given an extra baseball glove and the game was on.

CHAP+ER 2

MAN. What a game!

I hadn't really played baseball for a while. My arms and legs were sore but I sure needed the exercise though. It was a good thing I got out of the house today or I would've never met these guys. They were cooler than I thought.

During the game, I got to know them a little more. I actually gave them all nick names to remember them a lot better.

Jimmy was always in charge. He seemed pretty authoritative but he was mostly friendly. I really liked his personality so I called him "The Boss."

Bruce, on the other hand, was hilarious. That guy would make a joke out of anything but sometimes you'd laugh just cause of how stupid the joke was. I named this one "The Comedian."

Luis was "The Cocky Dude." Besides being cocky, that guy was always making sure his hair looked nice and neat. Mess with the guy's hair and you'd get a beat down and some Spanish verbal abuse.

Patrick was a frightened kind of guy. He wasn't really the talkative type either. I couldn't really tell you much about him. He was just "Mr. Shy."

Then came Larry. Oh. Man. This guy was "Grumpy." Everything bothered him. I am convinced he was a bully back in junior high. He seemed like the type who would pick a fight with anybody for anything. Every time he'd strike out, he would usually swing the bat at Patrick or throw the ball at Bruce just because. He missed of course, but that was still considered pretty dangerous. Thank God he didn't give me a hard time.

Note to self: Do Not Mess with Larry.

I just realized that I need one more guy to add to this picture and I could actually describe the seven dwarfs from Snow White.

Okay, lame joke.

It's not really funny because I was actually the 6th dwarf looking thing. I was the guy who's mostly scared of everything. Too bad Snow White was not around.

WRONG AGAIN.

As we all left the baseball field and headed out to the main street, we all shook hands and scheduled another game for the next day. As I walked away, I saw a cheerleading squad doing whatever cheerleaders do. There were a few guys there too. They wore these varsity letter jackets in black and gray.

Football players!

I guess there was a football team after all. Man was I glad to know that. I made it to the intersection to get back on Sunnyside Street. I looked back at the team and at the cheerleaders, and something made me gasp.

No, seriously, I actually gasped.

The cheerleading captain was really beautiful. She had long brown hair up in a ponytail and had a nice looking body, extremely curvaceous.

Wearing that cheerleading uniform made her look even more gorgeous.

I don't want to sound like a pervert but she was hot. I would totally kill just to know her name. I couldn't take my eyes off her. She was perfect.

One of the baseball players sneaked up behind me.

"That's Kate."

I spun around and suddenly my skin crawled when I came face to face with Larry.

Grumpy Larry.

Gulp.

I tried gulping again but my throat felt so dry like sandpaper.

"Who?" That was the only thing that came out of my mouth.

"Kate Anderson. That's her name." He continued pointing at the cheerleading captain.

"Oh? Umm, that's nice." I stammered, trying to sound completely normal but I was really making a joke of myself and Larry knew it. I saw it in his eyes, his cold blue eyes. He kept sizing me up as if trying to figure me out. Sort of like psychics do when they try to read your mind or maybe he wanted to bully me now.

Whatever it was, it was creeping me out. If running home scared was an option, this was the perfect opportunity. I tried making up a story. I wanted to say it in a way that wouldn't tick this guy off, so I spoke fast enough for him to understand but not so slow, so it wouldn't make me sound like a retard.

"Umm, I…got to go home now. Very imp—"

"Erick right?" He cut me off.

"Uh, yeah?"

"You're the new kid that moved next to my house. Sunnyside Street, right?"

"You live next to me?" I asked, surprised. My knees locked. My heart started racing kind of fast too.

"Uh huh. I saw you moving in about a month ago. Feels good to have someone new in town. Now I'll have a new buddy to hangout with all day. You did good today, by the way."

I was still trying to register what he just said about 50 thousand times in a few nanoseconds, but I only pictured Larry bullying me while I slept, sneaking in my room, breaking my window with a baseball bat, taking over my things and eating my dinner. I wanted to scream my lungs out.

I finally got a grip on myself and looked straight into his eyes and said, "I'm sorry. Come again?"

He took a few steps closer and lifted an eyebrow in confusion. "Are you okay, dude? Kate got your tongue?" he snickered.

I tried to fake laugh at his joke in total dismay.

"Are you planning to walk home?"

"Yeah, pretty much," I said quickly.

"I'll give you a ride home. I have a car. It's pretty fast!" he said with excitement. That was actually the first time I saw some type of emotion coming from this guy.

"Our houses are like a block away," I said.

"I know," he chuckled.

I didn't know if it was coming from the evil within or he was just laughing because he likes living a block away thing.

"I usually take the long way home, that way I can enjoy the ride a bit longer," he explained.

"Well at least gas money is the least of your worries," I said with a touch of sarcasm.

I really wanted to get home. It was getting late and I was exhausted.

"Look, Grump—I mean, uh, Larry?"

YIKES!

I almost committed suicide. I had to stop calling this guy Grumpy or it would totally bite me in the butt one day.

"Thanks for everything, really. I appreciate the ride but I really have to get home. Maybe you can show me around the neighborhood tomorrow," I said recovering from an

ALMOST GOT PUNCHED IN THE THROAT MOMENT.

"Sounds good," he replied.

I gave him a salute gesture. He nodded. I started walking away when he called out to me and said, "You should join the team when school starts next month. You are pretty good!"

I turned my head and smiled.

"I'll think about it"

It felt good to be home at last. My parents were out for the night, so I was home alone. I was so tired, my arms and legs felt like jelly. I didn't have any strength left for the night. As soon as I came in through that front door, I went straight into the kitchen and headed to the fridge. I made myself a gigantic ham and cheese sandwich, with lettuce and tomatoes. It was delicious!

Usually after a game like that, I would order Domino's pizza with my father and his friends and we would have a feast but I was starving this time. The sandwich filled me up pretty well. When I finished my sandwich, I went upstairs and showered. That also felt good. It actually felt like I just unloaded a building off my back. I wanted to stay in there all night. After showering, I put on my pajamas and went to bed.

Little by little, I was dozing off to dreamland. It was only 7 pm but I really didn't mind, since my body ached from such excessive exercise. I must have gotten out of shape during the summer and now I was paying the price. Then, for no particular reason, I started to feel kind of funny. I don't know what started it but I was beginning to feel anxious. I was nervous about something and I didn't know why, until I thought about the research. I tossed and turned for about 30 minutes, just thinking about it and couldn't sleep. I decided to get up and check my Facebook page.

Yeah, believe it or not I did have Facebook friends at least. Well, about 100 friends. That's a lot for me. Most of these people were my mom and dad's acquaintances. The rest were a few old friends from Cali, who don't even care about my existence.

Sad, I know.

Since my parents are constantly traveling due to their careers,

I barely get the chance to make friends much. Not to mention, my mother is so concerned about my wellbeing for some crazy reason that she does not want me to be out of her sight. She even had me homeschooled most of my life and it wasn't until this year that she decided it was time for me to socialize with other kids my age.

Thank God!

I sat at my desk and turned on my computer. I was scrolling through my feed and something caught my attention. A picture of my grandfather had just recently been posted by my grandmother. I looked at the picture carefully and again felt this sadness in my heart, this feeling of grief and sorrow.

How I missed that guy.

Losing him had been very tough for me and my family. I couldn't look at the picture any longer, so I decided to shut down the monitor.

When I did…

HOLY CRAP!

I don't know what I saw but it made the hair on the back of my neck stand up. I swear I saw these red glowing eyes outside my window. It was so quick, I stood up and looked outside my window but there was nothing there.

It was gone.

Whatever it was, it scared the living Jesus out of me. I must have been hallucinating. I was probably too tired and my mind was playing tricks or I was going nuts. I took a deep breath and as I got myself together, I went back to bed. I don't know what happened after that because I fell asleep till morning.

CHAPTER 3

Morning

IT WAS A BRIGHT sunny day on Sunnyside Street. There was a calming breeze coming from my window and it felt very soothing. I opened my eyes and looked at the time.

It was 8:38 am.

I'm usually not a morning person but today, I felt energized. I got out of bed and started doing my usual morning pushups.

YEEAWW!

Bad idea. That sure hurt. My body felt sore as if I ran into a truck.

Correction.

Like I was pushed off a moving truck and ran over by a train.

Not like I've ever been pushed off a truck and ran over by a train but you get the picture.

Someone knocked on my door.

"Come in," I said while doing one last push up.

"Morning, Erick." It was my mother.

"Morning, Mom," I said smiling. I stood up quickly. I shouldn't have done that.

GOOD LORD!

That hurt even more.

"I see you managed to put everything away before we did," she said, looking around with a smile.

"Please let this be our last move."

"I promise." She laughed, then got serious and looked down for a moment.

"What is it, Mom?"

"I was worried about you."

"Why?"

"I called your cell phone yesterday and left you voicemails."

"You did? I never got 'em," I said looking through my phone for any recent calls. I never heard the phone ring the day before. I guess I didn't have services by the school.

"Where were you, hun? I came home immediately thinking something might have happened to you but when I got home, I saw you went to bed early. Are you feeling alright? Is everything okay?"

"I was just a little tired that's all. How did it go at the GBI?" I said, hiding the pain.

"Well, I sat with my boss and I had a hard time convincing him but I told him, if we find what we're looking for, I will personally use the company's name as sponsors.

He looked pretty convinced after that." She walked towards my bed and sat.

"Breakfast is ready by the way. Would you like for me to bring it to you?"

I can't begin telling you how amazing my mother is. As overly protective as she is, she's still my mother. As she sat there, I only saw a guardian angel.

"It's all right. I'll be downstairs in a minute. Don't worry so much."

"So, where were you yesterday?" she asked again.

I was trying to avoid the question but since she asked, I had no other choice but to tell her the truth.

Kind of.

"I went out, uh…figured it would be a great idea to try to find my way around my new school. You know, since school starts next month," I stammered.

"What did you do?" she asked persistently. I guess that wasn't a good enough answer for her.

Swell.

I guess I'll have to tell her everything.

Kind of.

"Met some new friends at the school and we had a baseball game."

"Erick? When you play games without an adult to watch over you, you can get—"

"Mom? I'm not a little kid anymore" I glanced at her annoyed.

She must have sensed I was getting upset, so she stood up and slowly walked to the door. I must have hurt her feelings. As I watched her leave, I felt bad.

Like I said before, she only wants what's best for me, so I called out to her.

"I'm sorry, Mom, I just feel like I need to breathe once in a while. I might be just a little kid to you but I'm 16 years old now. I think I'm old enough to know how to take care of myself by now."

With those words, my mom burst into tears. Great, Now I made things worse.

I only tried to explain my reasons for reacting, but now, I also made her cry.

Way to go, Erick. You moron.

"Fair enough," she finally said.

HUH?

She turned around. I saw tears. She looked at me with these eyes of concern I'd never seen before.

"I know how you feel. I understand you more than you think I do. It's my fault you have not been able to socialize with your friends and enjoy your childhood years. I'm also responsible for not letting you make your own decisions either. You must forgive me Erick, but it is my duty to keep you safe."

She turned and left the room. For the first time she opened up to me. I felt a lot better knowing that we could both understand each other now.

I showered and went to get breakfast. As soon as I got downstairs and went into the kitchen, I saw my dad sitting at the kitchen table reading the daily news.

"Yo, wut up."

"Yo!" he said while putting down the newspaper and taking a sip of his coffee. I sat across from him. There were pancakes and some scrambled eggs waiting for me at the table. I don't know what had gotten into me but I guess exercising opens up your appetite.

Like big time.

I devoured the thing in seconds. When I finished, I turned to my dad who was staring at me. I shrugged and looked at his half-finished plate and asked, "Are you gonna eat that?"

He looked at my plate and then at me again. He chuckled. "What happened to you, dawg?"

"You don't wanna know. Long story."

"Try me," he said, still laughing.

"I met a few guys yesterday at my school. They were playing a game and I joined."

"You made friends! That's great! And then what happened?" he asked. I took a mouthful of my dad's pancake, chewed for a second, then before I said anything, I looked around making sure my mom wasn't listening.

"There was this girl."

"A girl?" he said out loud.

"Shhhh," I motioned for him to be quiet. "Her name is Kate Anderson."

"Well?" he said impatiently.

"She's gorgeous," I said. "The only thing is, she doesn't know me yet."

LOSER.

Of course, my dad was not going to call me that but I knew he was thinking it, by the way he kept staring.

"I'm guessing you saw her from afar and then there it is! Love at first sight. Am I right? He finally said, trying to understand.

"That's it, I guess."

"So what are you waiting for? Go talk to her. Take her out on a date or something," he encouraged.

"Soon," I said. "I think I might be heading back there again today, after mom goes to work that is."

"Right," he agreed.

"So? How's everything coming along?" I asked, still whispering.

"All we need is the money. I have a business proposal this morning with GBI. I sure hope they like it."

"Good luck," I said. He nodded.

I paused. for a moment. "Can I ask you something?"

"Shoot."

"It's totally off topic but do you know why Mom is the way she is with me?"

"What about her"

"You know, overprotective?"

"Oh, that."

"Oh what?" I asked.

My father was about to answer but he heard footsteps so he held his thoughts and continued reading the newspaper.

"Jack? Let's go. We're late," Mom said. She came to the kitchen table and gave me a goodbye kiss on the cheek. My dad stood up and patted me on the back as he walked towards the door with her.

Mom was the first one to walk out and soon after she did, Dad immediately turned to me and whispered, "Go get that Kate chick!" He gave me a sly smile and left.

Isn't he the coolest dad or what?

I was so ready to meet Kate. I was hoping she was at school today. I finished my plate, put on my sweater and headed out the door. When I opened it, I almost screamed like a girl.

What would you do if you opened your front door and there's a guy like Grumpy, standing there like some kind of FREAK?

"Larry? What the heck are you doing on my porch?" I said

while placing my hand on my chest. I felt like my heart was going to rip right through me.

"Nothing, just stopped by to say hello," he answered. "Besides, you did say you wanted me to show you around the neighborhood today. So here I am!"

"You could've knocked you know?" I said while letting him know this was a 'DUH' situation.

"Yes I know that, genius, but your parents were right outside, so I waited and there you go. Surprise!" He just stood there with his arms crossed behind his back, feet apart, like some kind of commando dude. Now I was frustrated, so I tried blowing him off.

"Not today Buddy. I've got to—"

"Check out Kate?" he finished, as if he knew all along where I was going, and he did, but I wasn't going to admit it.

"Umm, no. I was going to look for…a…store." I stammered trying to make something up.

"A store?" Suddenly he got serious. My frustration was gone. Now I started to panic. I thought he might choke me to death.

"Yeah, a store, uh, you know the ones you go and buy stuff at?"

"Erick? If you didn't want to hangout with me, you could've just said so." He turned and started walking away. I guess I must have over done it. The guy was only trying to be friendly, and here I was, complaining I don't have any friends.

Way to go, Erick.

Oh well. I guess my Kate will have to wait for another day. I tried catching up to him.

"Hey big guy?" I called out behind him. He stopped and slowly turned to look at me.

"Listen, I guess I started off the wrong way and my anxiety gets the best of me at times, that's all. You were right. I really wanted to see Kate."

He giggled. "Then hop in my ride, dude. I'll introduce ya!"

I had to smile. Did he really say he'd introduce me to Kate

Anderson? I was so looking forward to it. I guess Larry wasn't such a bad guy after all. I followed him to his car and it was wicked.

It had these red rims, which were so flawless that when the sun shined on them, it looked like his tires were on fire. When I got in it, I saw that it was one of those manual shift cars. I always wanted to drive one of those. I didn't have my driver's license yet but Craig taught me how to drive automatics when I was only 12.

The interior was also completely black and even had a plastic spider hanging from his rear view mirror. I guess black was his favorite color. Larry pushed the car key in the ignition and turned it on. I sat in the front passenger's seat and as soon as we drove off to school, which was only one block away, I started wishing Larry had taken the long way this time. I have to admit; the ride was totally awesome.

I imagined I was in one of those Fast and The Furious movies. The neighbors stared in awe as we drove by which only had me thinking that if Kate saw me riding in this baby, I could give her a good impression.

I know. I'm a dork. What can I say?

The football players from the other day were hanging outside the campus. There were like 10 of them. Some were smoking while the others drank root beer.

They were a wild bunch.

The guys from the baseball field were also there waiting on us. Larry parked the car a few yards away from where his team was, and as soon as we pulled over, they all rushed over to us.

Jimmy spoke first.

"What's up, big man?" He gave me a pound.

"Hey Jimmy! Hey guys!" I waved at them. They all waved back.

"You did pretty good yesterday," Patrick said.

"That's exactly what I told him," Larry said while he wrapped his right arm around my neck.

"You came back for another round then?" Luis asked with a smile.

"Actually he had other plans," Larry responded as he pointed at the football crew who were all staring back at us.

I overheard one of them utter something like, "Guys! Check it out. It's Larry!"

If they knew Larry, then that only meant I was hanging out with the popular kids.

Knowing that had me growing a lot more confidence. School had not started, yet I was already getting to know the big dogs.

"Sup, girls!" Larry said. I saw one of the guys walk down our way. This one was some brawny Johnny Bravo type of dude. Hair was even combed that way too. He had blonde hair and green eyes. He was also taller than me.

Christ! Everyone around me was a lot taller than me.

"Sup, home boy. Where the hell have you been? Still playing with them sissies?" he said, staring at my guys.

Ouch!

Did he just call Larry and his baseball team a bunch of sissies?

Larry didn't seem to get ticked off at that remark, so I'm guessing they were pals.

However, Jimmy and the rest of the gang were heated.

"When was the last time you won a game? 2 to 3 years ago?" Larry teased.

"Whatever man. Cut me some slack. We only lost once to the Patriots but that is not going to happen this year. Trust me."

"Sure. Till then, I'm better off playing with Jimmy than with you losers." They both chuckled, then the guy looked at me.

"Who's the new kid?" he asked.

"Mike, this is Erick. He's new in town. I'm giving him a ride around the block," Larry said, introducing me. I glanced at Mike. He didn't acknowledge me. He had a weird smile on his face.

Man, if he ever auditioned for the Freddy vs Jason movie, he'd so nail the Freddy character.

"He'll be going to this school?" Mike asked.

"Yeah, pretty much," Larry answered. "I'm trying to get him to join our baseball team too," He said.

"Actually, I wanted to play football this season," I said, joining the convo. Mike and Larry both glanced at me, surprised. It's like they weren't expecting me to say something.

"He spoke!" Mike teased. I guess that was more of an understatement.

"That's not all I can do," I said as a comeback.

"You hear that guys? This water boy here wants to join the team. Should we test him out?" Mike mocked. Everyone on the team laughed too. He still had that weird smile on his face. I wanted to punch it out of him.

"So? What do you say? I ain't got all day," I said annoyed. Larry laughed. He was enjoying this. My guys were surprised at my approach as well. Mike didn't like it though. He got serious.

"Okay then," he said while glaring at me. He got in my face, daunting me. I stood my ground and stared at Mike straight in the eye. I was ready for another comeback. One thing I was good at, I was witty.

"That's why I love this guy," Larry broke in, breaking the tension. "I've seen him play and I think he can beat you" Mike looked at Larry but kept glancing at me.

"Alright!" Mike finally said. He kept his cool. "We'll have a football game this Friday. If you want to prove your worth for this team, you better impress. This will be your time to shine, water boy," he said with a smirk. This time he was all business.

The first impression is the only thing that counts. I accepted the challenge. No way in hell was I going to back down from this one. No sir.

As Mike walked back to his guys, Larry winked at me proudly, then patted me on the back.

"That was awesome!" Bruce exclaimed.

"I can't wait for Friday," Jimmy said.

"Me neither," Larry also said.

We started heading back to the car. After I said my goodbyes to my friends, I stopped halfway. I was looking for someone.

Larry noticed.

"Ahh! That's right."

His eyes started darting around too, then he motioned me to get back in the car. He drove me around the school but unfortunately, there was no sign of Kate.

BUMMER.

"Looks like she isn't practicing today but lucky for you, I know what street she lives on," he said with a sly smile.

"Is there anything you don't know?" I said amazed.

"Well there is one thing. I just can't tell you yet or I'd have to kill you."

I couldn't tell if he was just joking or really serious about that comment. With Larry,

It was really hard to tell what he was thinking. Getting to know him was like detective work. He saw the frightened expression on my face and he chuckled.

"I'm just kidding, kid."

"Oh, okay, cool," I answered with a sudden relief. My cell phone rang.

I looked at the phone screen and it read: MOM.

I felt my stomach shrink. Was she back from work and found out I wasn't there again? I picked up the call and motioned to Larry not to speak.

"Hey, Mom."

"Hi, hun! GBI approved the loan!"

"That's fantastic!" I exclaimed, excited.

"Jack asked for us to pack immediately. Craig already made arrangements to go to Africa tomorrow morning."

"Do what?" I couldn't believe this. This can't be possible. This wasn't happening.

"By the way, your grandmother called," Mom continued. "She said she misses you very much. I'll see you soon, hun." She hung up. I only started blankly at nowhere for maybe 10 seconds. Larry drove but kept looking at me then back at the road.

"You're in trouble or something?" he asked.

"We have a problem, Larry."

"What? You gotta go home?"

"I do, but that's not the problem," I said quickly.

"What is it?"

"I won't be able to make it to the game on Friday."

"Oh?" Larry said, confused.

"My reputation is at stake here!" I shouted.

I didn't know if I was angry because once again, my father's career got in the way of me finally having a normal life or I was just nervous at the fact that I was going to partake in one of the biggest expeditions of all time and my father was going to become one of the most important figures in the entire history of history.

Larry and I didn't speak the whole way after the phone call. He must have sensed I was upset, so he left me alone in my thoughts. We finally arrived at my house and I got out of the car. I made my way back to the house slowly, when he finally shouted and said, "You know, if time is what you need, I can always ask Mike to change the game for another day or you could just change your mind and play baseball this season."

"I'll think about it," I said.

"And one more thing, chief."

I turned slowly. "When you're finally ready, come find me. We'll get the Others," he said.

He winked at me, then drove off to I don't know where. What was he talking about?

What Others? The only thing that was on my mind was the expedition. How long was it going to take? Was it going to take months? Was I going to be able to start school next month? Was this going to end up being a dead end, just like the rest of the excavations so far? All these questions kept popping in my head and were making my head hurt.

CHAP+ER 4

Home

AFTER SITTING IN MY room for about an hour contemplating my thoughts, I decided to start packing my bags. Maybe this way I would be able to forget about my issues and keep my mind busy.

Then right on cue, I heard something. Then there was a screeching sound, like if something was scratching the surface of a metal wall. I stopped what I was doing for a second and tried to listen carefully. I wanted to know where it was coming from. The sound stopped for a moment, then I heard it again. This time was louder.

Was it a burglar?

I slowly creeped towards the hallway and tried to listen closely. Then I heard it. The sound was so intense it hurt my teeth. I went back to my room and quickly scanned for something I could use to defend myself from whatever it was. I spotted my baseball bat, which was lying on the floor in a corner of my room.

YES!

I grabbed the bat and made my way to where the sound was coming from. As I kept creeping down the hallway towards my father's home office, I was a bundle of raw nerves. If anyone so much as farted, I was going to make a jump out a window and run like hell. The closer I got, the more my hands were shaking.

As I made my way to the door, I turned the doorknob. My cell phone rang. I freaked out. I glanced at the screen and it read: Unknown

I didn't pick up. But I turned my cellphone off. I sure didn't want to give away my location to whoever was in my house. I got myself together, took a few breaths and quickly pushed the door open.

The room was bright and shiny from the morning sun that came from the office window. No sound either. It was quiet. I went back to my room but then my cellphone rang again.

How?

I jumped and reached into my pocket and grabbed the phone. It was the same unknown caller again but that's not what freaked me out. It was the fact that it was still ringing even though it was off. I picked up and listened carefully. At first there was static, then there were whispers.

"Ethasus," I herd a voice say. The hair on the back of my neck stood up.

"Who's this?" I asked, frightened. "Larry? This isn't funny. It better not be you?" I said a little shaken.

Then the scratching sounds started again. This time it was so loud it hurt my ears.

Then I woke up.

CHRIST.

Thank god It was just a dream. I must have fallen asleep for a minute.

I got up from my bed and started walking around my room. I was still a little shaken. Then I started having the strangest feeling that I was being watched. I never experienced such a thing before but like I said, I felt like there was an unknown presence in my room. It was such an unnatural feeling. I looked around but there was no one there of course.

I heard a dog barking.

It was so loud and clear as if the animal was inside my house or in my head.

I ran out of my house.

Was I going insane? I think I was hallucinating. I thought of a billion possibilities and explanations but none would explain what just happened. How could I tell my parents? They'd freak out and take me away to a mental institution forever. I sat on my front porch for almost an hour when my parents were back.

I was so relieved.

"Erick? What are you doing out here?" Mom asked as she got out of the car.

"I was taking out the trash and decided to get some fresh air," I faltered with a lie and she believed me and we all went inside.

Hours later, my parents started packing too. This was my opportunity to ask my dad when we were coming back home. I went into his room.

"Dad?" I called. He looked up and stopped what he was doing. He looked pretty tense, I guess from stress. After all, this was the moment he was waiting for all his life.

"How long is it going to take?" I asked, as I sat on the edge of the bed.

"Don't know. It may take a while. It all depends."

"It depends on what?"

"On what we find and how long it will take."

"I thought you knew where Satu was."

"Yes, but those are just speculations from our previous findings, Erick. I can't really tell you for sure. At least not yet." Dad grabbed a pair of socks and a T-shirt and placed them on top of the bed.

"There is something that's been bothering me."

"What?"

"Nathan doesn't think Satu is in Africa. He insists he's on the island."

"That's strange. Maybe he knows something you don't," I said.

"Maybe, but lately he's been keeping things from me and Craig. I don't even know where he's getting these ideas from."

"What's he saying?"

"Things about a temple and an underground passage."

"An underground passage?" I exclaimed, puzzled.

"Yes, but the thing is, we've been to the island before and we've never found anything of that sort. As a matter of fact, we've spoken to the Detarrunians and they've never mentioned anything about a temple. I don't know where Nathan is getting this information from. I mean, it's definitely not coming from the manuscripts. All I know is that this is our last shot and I don't want to risk it. I don't want anybody interfering with this research," he said, lost in his thoughts.

It was really strange hearing my father speak that way about Nathan but I guess it was for a good reason.

"Do you think the Detarrunians might be hiding something?" I asked.

"I think so."

"For what reasons?"

He looked at me for a moment.

"Satu enjoyed torturing and killing innocent people and used to collect their souls, to gain more power from the underworld. Trading souls for power was one of his ways to gain immortality. For years, the Detarrunians were slaughtered and enslaved. They were tortured in the most horrific ways that some preferred to end their lives. In some cases, out of desperation, they sacrificed their loved ones to the gods, so that one day, they can be set free. The Detarrunians, to this day, still believe in this legend which is why they live in fear. They believe Satu will return with a vengeance and destroy mankind."

"That explains it." I said.

There was a long pause. I stood up for a moment and then turned to him.

"Dad?"

"Yes?" He looked up with a pair of shorts in his hands.

"Do I really have to go on this one?"

My father looked back at me. I wasn't sure if he was disappointed or sad. I can't believe I just asked him that either. I tried to make something up quickly.

"I start school soon" I said trying to fix the situation,

"I know," he finally answered in a sad voice. "If it takes longer, I'll arrange your flight back with Clara, but I'll have to stay behind. I won't get any more funds, so I really have to make this one work."

"What happens if you don't" I said, being realistic. My father took a moment to answer.

"If I don't, then I will not continue with this research anymore," he uttered.

Simple as that.

It's hard to believe that he was willing to give up everything. All of his findings, his passion, and hard work. I felt sorry for him, in a way, because he didn't have a choice.

We got so distracted talking about the research that we lost track of time. It was already 8 pm. I went downstairs and sat on the living room couch, thinking of all the negatives. The only thing that turned out to be good, at least for the moment, was Kate Anderson. That one moment, where I saw her for the first time. The most stunning cheerleading captain I had ever seen. Thinking about her, made me doze off and fall asleep till the next morning. That Monday morning, when I'd start an adventure, I'd never forget.

The Flight

Morning came fast. Really fast!

I don't remember falling asleep on the couch or how I ended up there in the first place but I slept really good. I heard a conversation coming from the kitchen. My parents were already up. I got up and headed to the kitchen where I met with my parents and their guests, Nathan and Craig.

"Well good morning, Erick," Nathan said with a welcoming smile.

"Morning, everyone."

"Morning," they all responded. I gave Craig a pound, then we did our signature handshake.

Dr. Craig Halloway. He sure was a funny dude. You'd never go bored with him. He was the type of guy that could find fun out of anything. Always energetic, and sports was his main hobby. He wouldn't stay still for one minute. We would go scuba diving, snowboarding, skydiving, exploring caves and rock climbing with my parents all the time. He was young too. Early thirties, built but average. He had black short hair and dark brown eyes. He'd been my dad's best friend since college. He usually got in trouble a lot with the cops and most definitely the girls. His weakness was the ladies. My mom hated him for that. She thought he was a bad influence for me. Craig and I actually grew really fond of each other. He always said I was the nephew he never had. So he fixed a few rebellious habits for my sake, but to me, he was still the old Craig no matter what.

"We need to get moving. Our flight is at 11 am," Nathan informed us.

After I ate breakfast and showered, my dad and I loaded the suitcases and all the equipment in Craig's truck. We left in Nathan's car and Craig drove the truck behind us. Everyone sat in their seats looking out through the windows, wordlessly, while I stared blankly at the road.

The Airport

We arrived at a private airport, which was about an hour away from home.

It wasn't like JFK, or La Guardia, which you go through bag checks, then check in, and wait for your plane at the terminal. This was a smaller and older airport. Instead of pavement, it had a long and narrow dirt runway, and three big airplane garages. There were two mini jets, and a chopper.

I recognized one of the planes. It was a 2007 Hawker 400xp.

The reason why I even knew that was because I used to collect toy planes when I was a kid.

Nathan pulled over by the smallest control tower I'd ever seen. There, we met up with another group of people. They were probably my father's archeological team. They seemed prepared and they carried a load of gear. There was a skinny tall woman who was very attractive. She had long blonde hair, pretty nice lips and amazing gray eyes. One of them was a short old man with gray hair. He looked fragile.

The other two looked like Robocops. When we all gathered by the plane, Nathan introduced us all, starting with 'Blondie'. Her name was Rebecca Taylor. She was a biochemist and a biological engineer. Her job was to study bacteria and other different living microorganisms that lived around dead bodies in tombs or something. Robocop-looking dudes were Joseph and Gregory. We weren't told what their job was in this project, but they looked like bodyguards to me. The old man's name was Matt. He was our pilot. How could someone his age possibly be allowed to navigate one of these Hawkers?

Then again, I wasn't the one pointing that out. He smiled politely as he introduced himself to us and asked, "Are we all here?"

"Yes," Nathan said.

"Where's the rest of the crew?"I asked.

During an expedition, you would need a mineralogist, some excavators, a chief of mechanics, and in case we got stuck in a cave or something, a demolition expert. Unfortunately, none of them were there. Even if they were, we weren't going to be able fit in that Hawker. The craft was designed for eight passengers.

"We will be taking a different flight" Craig Answered.

He took out his cellphone and started calling people. I overheard him talking to someone. "How's everything coming along? What? How come no one mentioned this to me before? Jesus Christ, Fred... Okay. Give me about an hour, I'll be there soon." Craig turned to my dad. "Alright guys. I have to go."

"What's going on?" my father asked.

"Apparently, everyone's flight was delayed, including mine, and it looks like we're gonna be stuck at JFK for a few hours. So, I guess we'll see you all in Africa," he said.

"Alright! Keep me posted."

Craig got in his truck and drove off. I heard a dog barking in the distance.

Matt smiled and faced the control tower.

"Here boy! Here Milo!" he called.

Out of nowhere, a huge brown and black German Shepherd came running up to him. It stood on his hind legs, and with his front paws, he leaned on Matt's chest. He started petting him lightly on his furry head. Oddly, this dog had the strangest eyes.

He had red eyes.

They seemed to glow, or maybe the sun was bouncing off in such a way, creating such effects. It was pretty cool.

"Ladies and gentleman, this is Milo," Matt introduced. I started petting the cute dog as well. I actually liked him!

"Will he be joining us?" I asked.

"Absolutely! Thought we could bring him along. He's highly trained and certified. He could be of great use tracking things. Definitely great to have, in case any of us gets lost or something."

Nathan spoke first and said, "We must leave now."

We loaded our gear and suitcases in the plane. I was the first one to enter the aircraft. After all these years, I've never had the chance to actually see one of these models from the inside. I was dumbfounded. The craft had a vertical squared oval cabin design with a flat cabin floor. There were center club seats, with seven individual passenger chairs. On the forward right hand side, there was a combination of refreshment galleys and baggage closets. There were sliding cockpit doors on each side.

I was so enjoying this.

My mother wasn't. She didn't make much conversation, or try bossing me around as usual. She looked worried. She found a seat and sat there quietly. I sat next to her and then asked her what was on her mind. She just stared at me expressionlessly.

"Mom?" I snapped my fingers and she finally focused.

"Huh?" she said. "What's the matter, hun?" she asked strangely.

"Just checking up on you. I kinda lost you there. Are you okay?" I asked, concerned.

"That woman," she said while looking at Blondie.

"Rebecca Taylor? What about her?"

"She looks familiar."

"You know her?"

"I don't know," she answered.

My dad joined us and sat across from us.

"Hey kiddo. Are you excited?

"Kinda."

"Well, I'm freaking out," he said nervously.

"Why?"

"If all goes well, we will find what we were looking for."

"Then why are you freaking out?"

"Because once I find him, I won't know what to do with him." He laughed. All I could do was smile back.

"Think about it, Erick; think about the many things we'll be able to learn from this ancient being."

"Or, you could just hand him over to area 51 and have them experiment with the thing. At the end of the day, the whole world will know about your research and you'll be a famous old man in our history books." I patted him on the shoulder as we both laughed, while Mom was still sitting silently, looking out the small window.

Blondie was already seated with the guards, while Matt was testing the engines. I heard him say over the speakers, "Good morning, everyone! This is your captain speaking, I will like for all passengers to take your seats, and strap yourselves in. We will be ready for departure in about 10 minutes."

Nathan came inside the craft with Milo on a leash. He took

the dog to the back of the plane and put him away in his cage. He then sat next to my dad.

Out of curiosity, I started observing all the crewmembers. Blondie and the bodyguards were having a secret conversation of their own in the back. Once in a while, they would look up, and stare at my dad, or at me. They definitely were talking about us.

Like, thanks for making it so obvious.

The engines turned on, and we started moving. The craft got in position at the start up lane, then we were cleared for takeoff.

The craft lifted up, and we were flying over New York City in minutes. I decided to just close my eyes and relax for a while.

CHAPTER 5

HOURS LATER

I GUESS I MUST have fallen asleep throughout the whole flight. When I opened my eyes and peeked through my window, the sun was already setting over the horizon.

That was super fast.

We were still another 2 hours away from Africa, and there was a huge time difference. It was probably like 6 pm already. I looked around the cabin, and found my mom and dad, sitting together, having a conversation with Nathan, and Blondie was on her laptop doing whatever biologists do.

I got up to use the restroom when Blondie called out to me.

"Hey, kid?"

I glanced at her. She smiled, and motioned for me to sit with her. I looked around, not sure if she actually meant for me to sit. Then I walked over and asked, "How can I help you, Miss Taylor?"

She looked up, smiling.

"Oh I just wanted to have a conversation with you. Do you mind?"

"No, not at all, Miss Taylor." I sat next to her, awkwardly.

"Please, call me Becky." She extended her hand to shake with mine. I took it, and introduced myself.

"My name is—"

"Erick," she finished. "Erick Ross."

"Uh, yeah." I smiled shyly.

"I know a lot about you."

The woman was gorgeous. Those beautiful gray eyes were locked on mine as she spoke. I'd never been intimidated by anybody before, but this time, I was.

"Perhaps Nathan or my father told you about me," I continued.

"Negative, I've been watching you and your father for quite some time now."

Well that was creepy.

She picked up her cup of coffee from the cup holder next to her seat and took a quick sip, with her eyes still locked on mine. She was not only making me nervous now but she was also making me very uncomfortable.

"Then you must be a fan," I said playfully but deep inside, I was thinking she was some kind of stalker.

"Haha, no not at all, Erick. You see, your father has a passion for this research, and finding Satu has been his only obsession."

"Yeah pretty much," I agreed.

"Does he know how important this research is to the world?"

"It will change history, if that is what you mean," I said.

"Not history, the future! Now that is my obsession." When she said those words, she made a hand gesture, as if to say 'The whole world depends on it'.

That sounded ominous in a way. Especially the part where she admitted spying on us all along.

"So you work for my father?" I asked, searching for answers.

"No. I work for Dr. Jeff."

"Oh."

"He needed an assistant. So, he brought me along with him on this research." She spoke in this professional manner that you would think she worked for the government or something.

Or did she?

"How long have you known Nathan?" I questioned. I wanted

to ask as many questions as I could. I wanted to know who she was and what's really her purpose in this research.

"Six years. We actually met at Glenwood Spring University."

This was very new to me. Nathan never mentioned her before. Perhaps she was indeed an old friend he happened to contact for this quest.

"I don't want to bore you with my stories." She continued, "Why don't we just talk about you? What are your thoughts about this Satu?"

I really didn't have an answer to that question. I took a deep breath to be able to choose my words carefully. Then I gave her a sideways look and said, "I've been asking myself that question for a while now. To my father, this is one of his greatest findings. Like you said before, it has been his obsession but I think this is wrong."

"Why is that?" She looked intrigued.

"Because it has taken my father almost 10 years to find this thing and it was hidden for a reason. I believe that reason is no good."

"So why won't you tell your father what you think?" She took another sip of her coffee.

"I can't."

"Why not?"

"If I do that, it will probably discourage him. I prefer to support him every way I can. It's the least I can do?" I gave her a sly smile.

"You're a good kid, Erick." She stopped typing and leaned closer to me. Her face was a few inches from mine. I was so nervous I didn't even breathe. It's like I forgot how to.

"What about The Chosen One?"

Just how much did she know about this research?

"Who?" I spluttered, blushing and shy.

She noticed my nervous expression so she backed away slowly.

"I think it will be extraordinary to find out where the Detarrunian hero is? Don't you think?"

"Most definitely!" I said, still a bit timid and confused. I wasn't sure what she was talking about anymore and I needed to use the restroom but I didn't want to be rude, so I excused myself and stood up. As I was about to head down the corridor, she grabbed my arm and said, smirking, "It was nice meeting you, Erick."

Really? What's with the smirk?

It totally reminded me of Larry. It's like they know something you don't.

I smiled ineptly.

She let go of my arm, and continued doing what she was doing on her laptop.

Was that her way of hitting on me?

I know I'm sexy and all, but really? She didn't have to go to those extremes. She could've just asked me out. Well actually, that's messing around with a minor, but I didn't mind. I mean, the lady was hot, but boy was she creepy. As I thought about what just happened, I walked down the corridor, and saw the German Shepherd in his cage. He was lying on his side, while he waved his tail in a very slow and calm motion, sort of like cats do.

As soon as I came close to him, he opened his eyes and stared at me. He was so adorable. I wanted to pet him. His red eyes kept looking right through me. Then I remembered the glowing red eyes I saw by my window a few days ago. The image in my head gave me chills, so I backed away and jogged quickly right into the restroom.

It felt good and relieving! But enough of that.

I got out of the restroom and walked back to my seat. Nathan was talking to Matt this time in the front cabin. Rebecca was still on her laptop and the guards were seated in the back eating our flight meals. My mother was asleep and my dad was reading a book alone. I thought this was the perfect opportunity to tell him about the strange dream I had the other day, and about Rebecca. Not about her hitting on me part, but about how very well informed she was about his research.

As I spoke to him, he listened quietly. When I finished, he crossed his arms around his chest and frowned. His mind was working. He usually does that when he's trying to figure something out. While his jaw muscles worked, he looked at me, then at nowhere in particular. Suddenly, he focused on me again and said, "How could she possibly know about The Chosen One?"

"Who's that?" I asked, still confused.

"The Chosen One was the only person who had the courage to rebel against Satu. He did not possess any powers nor was he as strong as him, but it was said that he built an army and defeated Satu in a massive battle. Soon after, the beast was defeated; Satu was imprisoned and taken away somewhere in the island, hidden forever so that no one was able to free him again."

"How come you never mentioned this before?" I asked, wanting to know more.

He looked at me for a second.

Our moment was crushed when our craft shifted a few degrees sideways and then we were hit by turbulence. It was as if we were being shot down by a ground assault. The lights were flickering and I saw a glimpse of my mom waking up and grabbing on to her arm rests. Dad and I held on tight too.

The turbulence stopped for a few seconds, then came back. We were flying straight through a storm. It was definitely cloudy out there. We were going to go through a hell of a flight.

"Everyone, this is your captain speaking. Fasten your seat belts," Matt spoke. "Please remain in your seats. We will be flying through heavy clouds for a few minutes. We will be landing on Detarru Island in about half an hour."

Wait a minute?

I turned to my father for answers. He was infuriated. I saw his frustration in his face but he held his thoughts till landing.

DETARRU ISLAND

It was nighttime on the island. How can I describe it?

It was beautiful!

Even in the night, I could still see the ocean under the bright moonlight, and make out the dark shadowy mountains. They looked like a long gigantic snake tail all across the island.

There was a nice gentle breeze, a warm tropical wind that blew in my face. We all got our gear and gathered at the center of what seemed like an outside terminal. There weren't any airports or security staff.

It was empty.

No tourists, no pedestrians, no buildings and no streetlights. It was completely isolated. It may have been an abandoned airport or maybe this island was just now developing into a modern society.

Heck would I know.

I'd never been to this island before. I remember paying attention to my science classes when I was homeschooled. I've always been a geek when it came down to planets, stars, Earth and the solar system but never heard anyone mention this place before.

I overheard my dad arguing with Nathan in the front of the craft. He wanted an explanation for landing on Detarru Island. However, Nathan was not answering his questions. My mother wasn't happy either.

"I need to show you something," Nathan said trying to convince my dad. "It's very important" Dad glanced at Mom and she started shaking her head.

"What is it?" Dad finally asked.

"I can't tell you, Jack. I have to show you in person. Otherwise, you won't believe me. If you don't like what you see, then we can head back and continue our flight to Africa," Nathan assured him.

Dad stood there for a while thinking. "Jesus, Nathan, you better make this quick, our crew is waiting for us," he finally said.

Nathan had a truck parked at the other side of the mini airport. He instructed us to wait for him at the center of the terminal. My dad volunteered to accompany him.

Matt asked me to let Milo out of his cage. I went back inside the plane but Milo was gone. The door was not forced or damaged, so who let the dog out? I looked all over the plane and searched the perimeter but there was no sign of him. I asked the crew if they let him out but none of them did.

That was very odd.

"Milo? Here, boy," Matt and I called.

No sign of him.

I heard the sound of a motor close by. It was Nathan and my dad. They were back in a black Cherokee. It was old but mobile.

"Okay everyone, hop in. Matt, we'll be back soon, so stay here. We won't take long," Nathan said.

"Got it," Matt replied.

"Is it really necessary to take the whole crew?" My father asked, annoyed.

"Absolutely! They all need to see this."

Matt continued searching for Milo while the rest of us got in the truck and made our way through a dirt road in the deep jungles of the island. Nathan was driving and Dad was in front with him. I sat between mom and Blondie, while the rest of the group were in the back seats.

"That's strange," my father said.

"What is?" Nathan replied.

"Where are the Detarrunians?"

"Somewhere up in the mountains or the village I suppose."

"Nathan, we are wasting time here. Why won't you—"

"Shhhh." He shushed him. "I'll tell you all about it when we get there. Stop being so stubborn, Jack."

We kept driving in the middle of the night on that long dark road. Nathan and my dad knew this place pretty well but it was an unknown territory for me. Nothing was visible, only a jungle and a dark road ahead. We continued on like this for about an hour, until Nathan pulled over and instructed us to get out of the truck.

We finally had arrived at our destination. However, we were

still in the middle of nowhere. Nathan walked to the back of his truck, opened the trunk, pulled out a few tools, then a 9mm gun.

Was he really planning to use that?

"Nathan?" my father uttered, worried.

I heard a squeal followed by a loud scream behind me. I looked over my shoulder and saw my mother with a knife to her neck.

HUH?

Gregory had control over her.

I was about to help her, when I felt two big arms wrap around me. It was a tight grip. Joseph had me in a bear hug.

"What is this? What's going on? Let us go!" my mom yelled. I turned to my father but Nathan had the gun pointed at him now. I didn't understand. What was going on?

"What the hell is this, Nathan?" my dad said in this voice I'd never heard before. He was angry. I guess that happens when you've trusted someone and they point a gun in your face.

Blondie walked towards Nathan and said, "Good job, Nathan. Just as we planned."

Just as they planned? They planned this? I thought we were friends. We trusted him. He was like family.

Rebecca took away all of our cellphones and smashed them by a tree.

"Now, Jack. If you know what's best for you, you'll come with us and do as you're told,"

Rebecca said.

"I'll do whatever you want but you must first let them go," my father conveyed.

"We both know we can't afford to do that. Right, Clara?" She looked at my mother.

Mom looked confused.

"What are you talking about? They have nothing to do with this. Let them go!" Dad demanded.

"That is not negotiable."

I tried to break free from Joseph's grip but he was too strong, so I came up with another strategy. I kicked down on his right knee and tried to get him on the groin but that was useless. He got pissed at my move so he spun me around so fast, I almost lost my balance. Then he grabbed me by the shirt and gave me a low blow kick to my stomach. I lost my breath. The impact had me bending down on my knees for air. While I was on my knees, Joseph grabbed both my arms and cuffed them behind my back.

Where did those come from?

"Easy with him. No need to harm the kid," Nathan said while helping me up. Rebecca turned on a flashlight and flashed it at my dad.

"What is it that you want?" he asked.

"We need you to help us find Satu. If you do, we will let your family go," Rebecca guaranteed.

"Seriously? That's the dumbest thing you could ask right now. Why do you think I'm going to Africa, you idiots?" Dad shot back.

"What if I told you Clara knows where he is?"

"What?" my dad exclaimed.

"Jack, you've been misled," Nathan assured him.

Rebecca walked over to my mom. "You can stop pretending now. We know everything," Rebecca said, as she turned the flashlight towards my mom now. She definitely looked like a deer in the headlights and she looked pale.

"Tell us the truth, Clara!" Rebecca snarled.

Mom stood there silently for a few seconds. She glanced at each and every one of us probably thinking about what she could possibly say.

"Start talking," Rebecca hissed. Nathan raised the gun at me now.

My heart stopped. I was so hurt. I did not expect this from Nathan.

"Okay. I'll tell you, but don't harm him," she pleaded.

Nathan lowered the gun for reassurance.

She took a deep breath and spoke very slowly. "Before The

Chosen One perished, he left a selected few in charge. They were called The Guardians. Their job was to guard the beast and protect the island from outsiders. They've done that for years and they will continue doing so for many generations to come. I myself am one of those guardians."

So if she was a guardian, then she must have been more than 100 years old, which didn't add up. This didn't make any sense. I don't think my dad registered what she just said either.

"You've got to be joking," he said. "Alright, guys. Look, I already knew my wife was a Detarrunian descendant. That was no big secret to me so I don't understand what the big deal is?" My father said, frustrated.

I personally didn't know my mom was a Detarrunian so that was a big shocker to me. Rebecca gave my dad a stern look, then turned to Nathan.

"I don't think he knows," she said.

"Apparently not," Nathan replied.

"Looks like she also forgot to mention one very important thing," Rebecca continued.

"Which is?"

While everyone was distracted, I tried to get Joseph off me. I got away from his grip again and landed on my back. The guy tried to come at me, but I kicked him hard on his right knee and he doubled over in pain. That was a bad move from his part though because I kicked him again in the head and he fell on the floor sideways.

Mom tried to fight Gregory off and my dad struggled to take the gun away from Nathan. Mom stomped on Gregory's foot and pushed the knife away from her throat. I thought she was going to run. Instead, she took the knife away from him, and started swinging it around, taunting him.

Wow! That threw me off a little.

Nathan and my dad were at it for a minute until the gun fell on the ground, close to Rebecca. She ran for it and picked it up. While they were still wrestling on the ground, I thought

Rebecca was going to shoot my dad for sure. My heart was in my throat.

She used the gun and delivered a blow to the back of my father's head. He collapsed to the ground unconscious.

"Dad?" I yelled.

"Do I have to do everything myself?" she said while rolling her eyes. She walked towards me.

I rolled to my side and tried to get on my feet, but she beat me to it and grabbed me by the back of my shirt. She stood me up with my back facing her, then pointed the gun to my face. Mom saw this and screamed, "Erick!"

"Do you want me to hurt him? Is that what you want?" Rebecca shouted. "Come with us or so help me God, I will shoot him."

Mom had tears in her eyes. She looked defeated. She always protected me but now there was nothing she could do.

"Carry him," Rebecca ordered Gregory, pointing at my dad.

Joseph grabbed my arm and pushed me forward. I was dragged to walk alongside them.

Why would Nathan betray us after so many years of friendship?

We walked through the jungle for another 10 minutes, when I saw an opening up ahead. Even in the dark, I could still make out that there was a clearing. I saw buildings also. Some were four stories high, and others looked like cottages. We were walking straight into the Detarrunian turf. The place was probably a city or a small town. What intrigued me about these buildings was their structure and the way they were built, sort of like castles. The architecture was really amazing.

There was a small entrance in the middle of a building and there was light coming from inside. Either the Detarrunians were waiting inside or they had no idea we were creeping outside their homes. The entrance seemed to lead downwards, like a cave. We remained in the dark areas where the Detarrunians wouldn't be able to see us, in case they were around.

I didn't see anyone though.

I thought this place would be a lot more secured. Where were these so-called guardians? Weren't they supposed to be guarding the place? Heck, if I were guarding Satu, security would've been a lot tighter than this.

As we kept creeping, I wondered if Nathan and Rebecca had gone psycho on us. However, they actually knew where they were going. That was no coincidence.

CHAP+ER 6

The Cave

WE ALL WENT THROUGH the small entry. The cave had stairs that led down to lower levels, which made it a little uncomfortable. We couldn't stand upright, and we had to squeeze through to wherever this entryway led to. I glanced at Gregory, who was struggling to squeeze through while carrying my dad.

Good for him. He deserved it.

I hoped that when Dad woke up, he'd be so pissed he'd punch him in the throat. I really wanted to see how good of a fight Gregory would put up then.

As for me, since my arms were handcuffed behind my back, I couldn't even hold on for safety. That made it even more uncomfortable. The thought of falling on my face and knocking all my teeth out had me a little worried. How would I be able to talk to Kate Anderson? I'd creep her out for good.

We were descending for about 5 minutes when we reached the basement, or the lower basement, or the basement under that one.

Whatever.

There was nothing great about this part of the cave. It just looked like any regular cave and it was pitch black. The only lights that were coming through were from the torches that were scattered in every corner of the place. The good thing was that we could finally stand up straight.

Nathan turned to us and gestured to stay quiet, then he continued walking and we followed quietly. We made a few turns every so often. Some instances, we would come across two or three passageways. Rebecca chose the right one every time, thank God. I wonder what would happen if we went the wrong way? Perhaps hit a dead end or get lost in here; after all, this place was a maze.

We kept coming across different doors that were locked. There were about six of them, and you needed some weird circular keys to open them too. Somehow, Rebecca had all six keys. Thank God for that too.

I was getting tired though. Having your hands handcuffed for a long time, without being able to use them, could get tiring. It was also hurting my wrists, so I stopped. Everyone turned to face me, except for my dad. He was still in dreamland.

"What is it now?" Rebecca asked, taking a deep breath, annoyed.

"Is it possible to use my hands again?"

She walked towards me and started taking the cuffs off me. "If you do anything crazy, I won't think twice about handcuffing you again."

"Sounds good to me," I said, relieved.

"And no talking either or I'll gag you too, is that clear?" She gave me a mean stare with those intimidating gray eyes of hers. I nodded very slowly.

Jesus, it felt good to have my arms back though. I rubbed my wrists from the pain. They were bruised up a little.

We continued walking.

I felt a warm draft. Yet it felt relieving, since we'd been underground for a while now. There was also this irritating sound that got louder and louder every step of the way. What the heck was it? It sounded like steel.

We hit a dead end and I thought we were going to turn back around and head another way, but Nathan kept walking towards a wall. Actually, it wasn't a wall. It was a steel door, and the strange sounds were coming from behind it too. I was scared and excited at the same time. My dad would've loved to see this. All these years of hard work, just to find out that he'd only end up betrayed by his best friend.

That would hurt.

I turned to Gregory who still carried him, and I wished I was able wake him.

As we walked near the steel door, I saw ancient engravings on it and it had beautiful designs. It had carved drawings and Detarrunian hieroglyphics. On one side, it had a drawing of a king. The king had a skull mask on, and was sitting on his throne, while looking down at his people or Detarrunians. I'm guessing the king was Satu. Every drawing was different, and it was expressing the history of the island.

It was fascinating!

There were two levers on each side of the heavy set of doors. Sort of like those 'Indiana Jones' type of mechanisms that take two people to open. You'd have to turn with it 360 degrees, a few times, until it fully opened.

"We have to use these," Nathan instructed, pointing at the two levers. "Hey, Joseph? Give me a hand here," he called.

Joseph walked up and positioned himself next to the right revolving handle. Nathan went to the left lever, and together they pushed as hard as they could. It wasn't budging. It took more than just two people. Nathan called me and Gregory over to give them a hand. I stood next to Nathan. Gregory gently put my dad on the ground, then joined Joseph. When the doors opened up a few inches, a warm wind blew in our faces. Bright lights hit us instantly. I had to cover my eyes for a minute, since we'd been in the dark for a while. As I tried to adjust to the brightness, I saw a spectrum of light; it had purple, orange, red, green, blue, and yellow. I imagined walking into a 'Skittles' world.

If it hadn't been for our current situation, I would've thought that was funny, but this was no joke. This was real.

The spectrum lit up the room for a few seconds, and then it

died off. We kept pushing and going in circles, until the doors fully opened. We all stopped to catch our breaths, but we were staggered at what was behind those huge metal doors.

It was a monumental sculpture made out of bronze. I went to get a closer look at such immense and beautiful artwork, then realized that I'd seen it before. It took a while to figure out what I was staring at. My knees locked.

Dante's Inferno!

The actual Gates from 'The Divine Comedy'. It told the story of a guy named Dante and his journey to Inferno, Purgatory, and Paradise. I'd seen these doors before, at the Metropolitan Museum in New York City, but the one at the museum was only a copy. My dad told me there were actually seven gates, each located in every continent of the world.

Now that I think of it, this was no continent. This was an island, which meant that Satu had an eighth gate all to himself.

"This is it! This is why I needed all of you here!" Nathan said, excited.

I heard moaning. Dad was regaining consciousness. He rubbed the back of his head, then he rolled to his feet very slowly, not to fall backwards and knock himself out again. He turned to us, but never said a word, because his eyes were fixed on the huge gates behind us.

His mouth dropped. He could not believe it. It was so mesmerizing for him, as it was for all of us. He slowly made his way to the gates and stared at it in wonder. I could only imagine what was going through his mind at that moment. He turned to us, and pointing at the doors, announced: "The Gates of Hell." We all looked at the gates in bewilderment. "These doors divide two different worlds," he continued. "Our world, and the underworld."

"I thought it was a myth," I said in disagreement.

"It isn't!" Dad responded quickly. "The manuscripts state that Satu used this portal to take those slaughtered souls into the underworld. Satu wanted more power and immortality, so he created his own VIP access."

"So then where's the beast?" I asked.

Rebecca gave me a sideways look. Every once in a while she would turn to face me, and she just stared at me for no reason at all. Either she was still flirting, or she was looking at me for answers but I was just as lost as she was.

"Clearly, he is somewhere in Africa, but Nathan insisted on coming here anyway," Dad explained.

"They're all lies, Jack," Nathan replied.

"What is it with you and—"

"Jack, listen to me. The answers are here, on this island. They've always been. These texts are only going to keep us going in circles, with false information. This is exactly what the Detarrunians want. They are trying to keep us from the real truth."

"What truth?" My father asked dreadfully. He wanted to know where Nathan was going with this.

"Satu is in the underworld!" Nathan said, pointing at the gates. My dad stayed quiet. It's like he was just slapped in the face with facts, but he was still in denial and wasn't really buying it.

"How do we get him out?" he asked.

"Only Satu was able to walk through them. No mortals were allowed. If we were to walk through these gates, we wouldn't be able to come back out," Nathan answered with another very important fact. "The Chosen One purposely dragged him in there to make sure no one was able to get him out for good. However, Rebecca mentioned there might be another way."

"With The Book of Mythos!" Rebecca declared.

Mom glared at her, shaken. "You can't possibly consider that," she said, frightened.

"If we read off that book, we might be able to set him free and he'll walk out of there on his own," Rebecca finished simply, ignoring my mother.

"And if he doesn't?"

"Let's just hope it doesn't come to that."

"Where is this book?" Dad questioned, interested, wanting to know more.

"The book is hidden in a temple. Only a guardian can show us the way," Nathan said. Rebecca and Nathan both turned to my mom. She knew where Satu was all along, and never bothered telling my dad.

Okay, I hated everything about this research now more than ever.

"Let's get moving!" Rebecca shouted.

We all followed my mom back outside quietly. We were all traumatized from everything that transpired, from the moment we set foot on this island. We walked about 2 miles before we found ourselves in front of a massive mountain. We hiked it no problem.

Yeah right.

Hiking in the middle of the night can get you steaming mad from frustration. Especially when you're stumbling over rocks every 2 seconds. Oh, and not to mention, when it's pitch black and you don't know if you're stepping in mud, quicksand, or in an endless pit.

What are the odds?

We'd already proven that The Gates of Hell were real. Seconds later, that a dead guy was easy to bring back to life, thanks to some witch book. Not to mention, my mother was a Detarrunian descendant and most importantly, a 100-year-old guardian. I mean, bumping into a prehistoric dinosaur wouldn't be a problem now, would it?

I kept imagining the impossible while we ascended to the very top of the mountain. The first thing we saw were these staircases that were made out of white stones. They were old, but still intact. Carefully, we made it to the top of the stairs, and to the very top of the mountain this time. There, we saw this astounding monument, which was also made out of white stones. The front of the temple had these enormous white pillars that looked ruined, but they still sustained in place.

"The Temple of Ethasus!" Nathan stated for everyone to hear. "Perhaps now a sacred temple for prayers."

"Ethasus?" I asked in awe.

"According to ancient mythology, Ethasus was The Chosen One's name," Dad said. As my father explained that theory, I got lost in my own thoughts again.

Where had I heard that name before?

It sounded awfully familiar. I probably read about it somewhere. It sure rang a bell. I didn't realize that the group started walking again, towards the temple, when my thoughts were rudely interrupted by one of Blondie's goons. He grabbed me by the back of my neck violently. I couldn't tell which of the two goons had me but he sure had a grip. He then shoved me with such force I tripped over my own foot and fell on my stomach. I almost knocked myself out.

OUCH.

I looked over my shoulder and saw Joseph standing there like a felonious moron, enjoying that.

"Keep moving," he sneered.

DUMB TWIT.

He was probably still mad at me for kicking him in the face a few hours ago. Oh well.

The group stopped and saw me on the floor. Nathan slowly spoke in this calm, but yet menacing voice.

"I told you not to harm him, didn't I?"

"Yeah, but he wanted to escape," he answered with a terrible lie.

"Don't touch him again, or you will pay with your life," Rebecca said flatly.

I sure hope he understood that. He nodded, lifted me up and dragged me to join the others. This time, we headed towards the temple.

The Temple of Ethasus

Have you ever been to one of the great cathedrals? If you have, then you have a pretty good idea of how beautiful this temple was. It was identical in a way, but this one was way more astounding. It had amazing marble walls and floors. The little moonlight we got from the windows was bright enough to see the interior's structure in detail. The whole temple was filled with sculptures. There were also five statues in every corner, which represented valiant warriors who fought for the island. They looked like archangels.

In every window, there were colorful drawings in stained glass, showing their cause and history. At the center of the temple, at the end of the open and spacious hallway, there was an altar. On top of it stood another statue. As soon as we got near it, we stopped and gazed. It was the statue of Ethasus. The statue had angel wings and it was holding a book in his right hand, while his other hand held a sword and seemed to be pointing up at something. As my dad studied the statue, I could see his eyes were wide open with curiosity.

"I've never been to this part of the island before," my dad spoke. "You were right about everything, Nathan! The Detarrunians were keeping the truth from us."

Every time he would turn to my mother, she would stare back at him uncomfortably. I can't blame her. The guilt of hiding the truth from my dad for all these years must have been killing her inside.

"Look!" Nathan exclaimed facing the statue. "It seems to be pointing up at something." We all looked up.

High above on the ceiling were six colorful circles. They were purple, orange, red, green, blue, and yellow. Same spectrum of colors that appeared at the gates. I wondered what they meant.

"What is it pointing to?" Nathan asked, looking at my mother.

"Other worlds," she answered.

"So what now?"

"We have to put them in order. Once we figure out the sequence, a secret passageway will open up. The passage to The Book of Mythos, and The Chosen One's resting place."

WOW!

The Detarrunian hero was here all along. I turned to my father and he also looked baffled to hear that. He could not believe The Chosen One's body was hidden on this island too. Somehow Rebecca and Nathan didn't seem to care. They were more focused on finding Satu instead.

"Well that's easy!" Nathan said. "Just like Dante, these circles must represent the underworlds. Inferno, Purgatory, Paradise, Hell, Earth and Heaven."

"Let her do it, so that we can get to the book already," Rebecca demanded.

Mom got the message.

She walked to the back of the statue. Behind it, there were some small controls or a mechanism of some sort. She turned one of them, and the red circle moved to the front. She turned another panel, and then the orange circle moved. Then the yellow, then green, blue and purple. As soon as they were all in order, they joined together, and fused into one flamboyant white circle.

We heard a roaring sound, which was coming from the statue. The hand with the sword that was pointing up, was now pointing straight ahead, horizontally. It was pointing at a door that appeared from behind the walls. That must be the secret passage Mom was talking about.

"This is it! The book is inside. Follow me," Mom asserted.

We all followed.

The passage was inside the walls and it had beautiful drawings and artwork all around. There was a horrible stench, though. It smelled like the dead and it was making me nauseous.

There were a few stairs that led to a lower level that was built underground, similar to the cave in the Detarrunian village. It had torches scattered all around.

We finally came across what looked like a sarcophagus. It was made out of pure gold and there was a torch on the wall illuminating it.

The Chosen One's resting place.

As we looked around, we noticed that we were surrounded by thousands of mummified bodies in catacombs. It was like an underground cemetery.

This island was definitely a city of the dead. It sure gave me the creeps.

Nathan and my dad walked up to the golden sarcophagus. They both examined it, and together they pushed the top off. As soon as the top came off, a weird mist spewed out of it.

That's disgusting.

We got closer to peek inside, and saw that there was an ancient book that was made out of steel. In the middle of the book there was this strange keyhole, and in every corner, it had circles. Each one had the same colors as the ones in the ceiling back in the temple.

Nathan picked up the book, but he couldn't open it.

A thought made my skin crawl.

"Guys? Th—the body!" I mumbled.

"Yeah, what about it?" Nathan asked, still examining the book.

"It's missing." I visualized The Chosen One's corpse, ready to feed on my flesh.

Ok, Erick. Snap out of it.

"The Book of Mythos is cursed," my mom stated, thankfully distracting me from my terrifying imagination. "It's sealed with dark magic. The only way of opening the book would be with a special key."

Nathan pulled something out of his left pocket.

It was a golden, antique and rusty skeleton key. It had the Detarrunian markings on it, and a small scary looking skull.

"What is that?" my dad probed him as he stared, perplexed.

Mom stepped back in terror when she realized that Nathan had the key. I think I heard her murmur something.

"You see Jack? While you and Craig were busy trying to track down Satu in Africa, I've been searching the island very thoroughly. You wouldn't believe the things I found out about this place!" Nathan exclaimed.

"How did you find out about Clara?" my father asked, wanting to know how much he knew.

"6 years ago, when I met Rebecca at Glenwood Spring University, she told me all about you and your family."

"But, how would she know all this information about the island?" He was still puzzled.

"Because I am also a Detarrunian," Rebecca answered.

Well this was getting better and better.

"A few years ago, I was wrongly accused of being a spy and a traitor, just because I had a different standpoint about the guardian's ideals. They thought I was a threat, so I was exiled from the island forever. Since that day, I've sought vengeance, and rebelled against the guardians by joining The Satunian tribes." We were all bewildered.

"I remember now. It was you?" my mom recalled. "You were the one trying to steal The Book of Mythos."

"I wasn't stealing it. I just wanted to do research on it, in the name of science. Gaining the knowledge that's contained in this book will make you view the world a different way. It is why I finally understood Satu's purpose and the reason why he did what he did."

"You're just sick in the head!" my mother yelled. "There's nothing right about that demon, and you know it!"

"Who are these Satunians?" my dad asked.

"We've been dealing with an opposing side of the tribe, which believes that Satu's methods are the way to salvation. They are convinced that bloodshed will satisfy the gods, but they're wrong. There can never be too much evil or it will bring an instability on Earth. There have been many battles fought between both groups and luckily we've succeeded each time," Mom informed us.

"You guys won't be so lucky next time. You have no idea what's coming to you. You wait," Rebecca said with a hateful grin.

Nathan placed the rusty skeleton key in the lock and then turned it. The colorful circles started glowing. We all heard a click sound, followed by an echo of voices.

"Guys? We should get out of here," I suggested.

After a few seconds the voices stopped. We were all silent for a moment. At one point, I thought I heard my own heartbeat.

Nathan opened the book and started flipping through the pages that were made out of black steel.

Mom was tense. Something made her very uneasy. She glanced at my dad, who happened to be as troubled as she was.

"I found it!" Nathan exclaimed.

"Let me see" Rebecca said quickly as she examined the page. Her eyes were wide in wonder. She smiled.

"We did it!" she said. "We actually did it!"

"Don't do this. You don't know what you're getting yourselves into," my mother warned again. "You don't know this monster. He's going to destroy us all."

They ignored her warnings.

I took advantage of this opportunity and walked towards her.

"Why didn't you tell me?" I whispered. She slowly turned to me with those sad eyes.

"To protect you!"

"Protect me from what? From who?"

My entire life, I'd been on lockdown, and never had a normal life because of her secret identity and this stupid research. Now I wanted answers, no more lies. I wanted the truth, and I wanted to know everything.

"The Satunians threatened to kill you if I didn't give them what they wanted. It is why I couldn't let you out of my sight."

"Bring him here," Rebecca ordered as she pointed to me. Gregory grabbed my arm and pulled me towards her. Gregory handcuffed me again, but with my hands in front.

"What now?" I asked in dismay. I was already a raw nerve.

When she turned to Nathan to hand him the book back, I took advantage of that opportunity. I pulled away from Rebecca and made a run for it. I ran down the hallway, towards the entrance and heard Mom shouting, "Run, Erick!"

But before I could reach the door, I was tackled to the ground.

Joseph picked me up on his shoulders and flung me back down on the floor, hard. I almost suffered a head concussion from that one. He picked me up again by my collar, and was about to deck me in the face with his fist, but I was too quick for this guy. I bent my knees, and got him in the privates.

He screeched in pain.

As I tried to move away from him, Gregory grabbed me from behind in a bear hug. I couldn't use my hands, since they were handcuffed in front of me, but I kicked backwards.

No luck, he dodged all my kicks. Joseph recovered and came at me too.

It was useless.

Joseph clutched his fist tight and bashed me in the stomach. Dad saw this and ran towards Joseph to save me. Joseph was going to take another swing at me when the unexplainable happened.

CHAPTER 7

BEFORE MY DAD COULD save me, Rebecca grabbed her gun and shot Joseph right in the head with no regrets or remorse. My mom screamed and my dad fell on one knee when he heard the gunshot as a reaction, and covered his head. I just watched in fear as Joseph's lifeless body dropped to the ground.

Everything felt like slow motion.

My head was spinning and I wanted to puke. Gregory jerked me forward. He didn't appear to care much that his partner was shot dead.

"Why would you kill him?" I screamed at her with my voice cracking.

"He had it coming," Rebecca replied. "I warned him not to lay a hand on you, he did anyway."

"He might have crossed the line, but he did not deserve to die like this," I said, still disturbed.

Nathan and Rebecca both exchanged looks.

"Clara? You never told him?" Nathan asked, concerned.

"Tell me what?" I asked, lightheaded.

Nathan looked straight into my eyes, placed a hand on my shoulder.

"You are Ethasus, silly!" he said with a chuckle.

HUH?

I turned to my parents, waiting for an explanation.

"Wait, you can't possibly think that my son is—" My dad

didn't finish the sentence. He glanced at me like if I was a stranger. It was like he didn't even know who I was anymore.

HECK, I didn't even know who I was anymore.

My mom didn't say a word. That only confirmed that it was true.

There's no way I could be some ancient super hero.

"Nathan? I don't know where you're getting this ridiculous information from, but this is absolutely outrageous. You need to stop this madness right now," my father ordered, heated.

My dad was right, this was too much for me, and my head was about to explode.

"Why would I lie about this?" Nathan blurted out, sounding annoyed.

My dad turned to my mother, pleading for answers.

"They're right, Jack," she finally said.

"How is this even possible? I thought that—Is Erick even our child?"

"It's complicated," my mom stammered. "The guardians were afraid you'd find out about Ethasus. So, in order to protect him, we tried bringing him back to life, with The Book of Mythos. Instead, I gave birth to him and he was just strangely reborn again. I had him genetically tested several times and oddly, we are his biological parents."

Yeah, I'm definitely going to lock myself in a mental institution once I get back to New York.

"What in the world were you thinking, Clara? Why would you keep this from me?" Dad shouted angrily.

"How was I supposed to explain all of this craziness to you and our son, Jack?"

As Mom and Dad argued, we made our way out of the temple.

I was taken again, and I felt hopeless.

Nathan and Gregory were still dragging me. I was tired of resisting by now, so I gave up on trying to get free. I wanted to yell my lungs out and alert the Detarrunians, but there was no one around. There was still no sign of them.

Where were they?

We made it back to the cave and down to The Gates of Hell again.

Rebecca opened The Book of Mythos.

"You guys have to stop. I'm begging you," Mom pleaded. "Once he's free, do you really think you'll be able to control this demon? He'll kill us all."

Rebecca started reading out loud, ignoring my mom's warnings. She was shouting Detarrunian words.

We heard a roaring sound and the sound of metal but this time it was coming from the gates.

The spectrum of light came back and it was brighter than ever. This time, it was distorted. It sure looked like we screwed something up. The Gates came to life and opened instantly. There was nothing but pure darkness on the other side. Nathan walked up to the gates with his flashlight. It was like a black hole. Even after shining the light, it was still dark.

"You think he'll walk out of there?" Dad asked.

"We can only hope and see," Nathan answered.

Rebecca started flipping through the pages again. "There! This is it. This better work!" She started reading. She read something out loud, then we heard voices. It was the same voices we heard at the temple. There were screams too. I couldn't really say it was human. They sounded more supernatural to me and they were coming from inside the gates. Whatever was in there didn't sound friendly. I really wanted to go home.

We heard thunder outside. It started raining hard. Raindrops were heard hitting the ground and echoed all around the cave.

We all thought Satu would crawl out of there by then. That image, of course, would be terrifying to me. 10 minutes passed and still no Satu. We thought something went wrong.

What a relief.

"It didn't work," Nathan said. "There has to be a mistake."

"Well, if Ethasus put him in there, I think he should be the one to get him out," Rebecca suggested.

DO WHAT?

"Are you mad?" Dad shouted, not considering the idea.

"You're right! Ethasus is the only one who has the ability to walk through those gates," Nathan said.

"You can't possibly be considering this, Nathan!" My mother exclaimed.

"There is no other way."

"Of course there are other ways, but definitely not by using my son as bait!" Dad yelled at him.

"The spirits of the dark will kill him, Nathan! Erick isn't as strong," Mom shouted.

Nathan thought about what she had said for a minute.

"We can't wait any longer. We need to get off this island before the locals find us," Rebecca affirmed. Nathan turned to me. He was having second thoughts.

"I'm sorry, Erick, but she's right. You are going to have to go in there," .

I looked at the gates in horror. I started trembling from fear and began backing up slowly.

"I will not allow this!" my dad screamed. He was pissed off again.

"Relax, Jack, if anything goes wrong, he can just turn around and walk back out. It shouldn't be that hard," Nathan concluded with a theory no one had ever tried before.

I backed away in terror, refusing to go.

Rebecca cocked her gun, hit my mother in the face and pointed the gun at my parents.

"Start walking, kid."

I've never despised anyone so much before in my whole life.

Gregory grabbed me and pushed me towards the gates. I was yelling for my life and pleading for mercy.

"Wait!" Nathan shouted.

Nathan walked towards me. He stood there examining the gates, and then took off my handcuffs.

"Here, take this flashlight with you just in case."

Just in case huh?

I was really furious, and tired of being pushed around and lied to. I stood there staring at The Gates of Hell, then turned back to my parents. My father was enraged while my mother was devastated. I could see it in her eyes.

I looked back at Nathan.

"I'm sorry," he said.

"You've disappointed me," I responded with disgust.

His eyes got watery and his face filled with shame. My words pierced right through his heart. He only looked down at the floor in embarrassment. I thought about my chances of surviving this, but I didn't even know what was on the other side of those gates. All I knew was that if I didn't comply, my parents were going to get hurt.

I couldn't let that happen.

I took a deep breath, closed my eyes and walked right inside The Gates of Hell.

Inferno

I can't describe it. It was just as I imagined, but a million times worse. It's not like you could really tell what any of it is. It just is.

A living nightmare.

There are many more monstrosities. It's darker, colder, and deeper than any abyss. There are a lot more flesh eating demons. A lot of angrier, lost, tormented, and tortured souls. It is more evil than the devil himself.

I tried to go back, many times. I wished there was another way back to my family, but the portals won't allow it. Somehow the gates were sealed shut, and it seems like I'll never be able to get back.

I don't know how long I've been in here either. There's no such thing as time in the underworld. I could've been in here for 50 years, or a whole eternity. Who knows?

No one talks to me. Not even the dark entities of hell. They won't help me either. I've been captured, many times, by these red-faced, skull-looking things. This place is swarming with these bloodthirsty creatures. They have legs and arms, but they run like animals. They don't even have eyeballs either, just empty eye sockets.

I call these creatures hollows.

I keep asking myself, how are they able to see me?

They have these nails that are 3 inches long, which they use to attack. It hurts every time. It isn't as painful as when they use their long sharp teeth to bite on my flesh and try to suck my blood. They've tortured me relentlessly. Luckily, I've managed to escape their flaming hot grasp every time. All I could do is run like hell.

Kind of ironic isn't it?

Either I'm running, or hiding under rocks and behind walls. It doesn't really matter, because I get caught anyway. I've been lucky enough not to get caught by the bigger demons. The bigger they are, the more likely I am to get eaten. I don't even know how to get back to the gates anymore. I lost my flashlight when I was attacked the first time. I don't even know where Satu is.

How can I find him? And where do I start?

Being in here has taken my will to live. It has made me miserable. My body, my being, my soul, everything. It's like a dark cloud surrounding me, drowning me little by little. It's painful.

You don't sleep, you don't eat. Nothing is normal about this God forsaken place. I've asked them to kill me. I've been wanting to end this, but they won't do it. It satisfies them to have me here trapped, and hopeless.

I've been called by the name of Ethasus. Even spoken to as The Chosen One. That is why I'm treated the worst way you could ever imagine. Every day, I keep reminding myself of who I am, because as days go by, I keep forgetting even who my parents were and who Erick was.

Those memories are what keeps me sane, because there's no one to trust, and I'm alone.

I've lost all Hope.

CHAPTER 8

DETARRU ISLAND

REBECCA, NATHAN AND ERICK's parents waited impatiently by The Gates of Hell. An hour passed and there was still no sign of Erick.

"We need to head back to the terminal. We can't stay here much longer," Rebecca declared.

"The hell with that! We're not going anywhere until Erick is back," Jack demanded.

"He's right. We can't just leave him here," Nathan exclaimed.

"Maybe he got lost and now he can't find his way back," Jack said.

"What if he's dead?" Rebecca asked.

She ticked Jack and Clara off.

"Watch what you say!" Clara shouted angrily. She started pacing from frustration.

Her son was trapped in there, with no way out, and there was nothing she could do.

They all waited impatiently for Erick to come back.

INFERNO

I managed to escape!

I think.

I haven't been caught for days. I don't know where I ran off to though. This place didn't look anything like where I used to be. I didn't see any spirits or demons around here either. This side is a lot darker and scarier than the other. You don't know how sick I am of this place. You're probably sick of me too, and I don't blame you. You might be asking yourselves; what the heck is wrong with me?

Well, for starters, I can't help it, I've tried. I have to vent, one way or another. You'd probably feel the same way, if you were in my shoes.

I heard something.

I just saw something fly over my head. I can't make out what it is.

What is that thing?

It's growling at me and flying towards me now.

Oh no! I've been spotted. This time by one of the big demons. This is not good. If I don't get out of here, he's going to eat me.

He flew over my head. He missed my head by an inch. I ran the other way, and he came after me. I ran, and ran in fear.

THAT DOES IT.

I'm tired of being chased around. If he was going to eat me, then I'm going to make him work for his meal. I came to a halt, looked back at the thing and saw he was about 8 feet tall.

YIKES!

He was tall. Very tall.

He had fangs like teeth that were about 6 inches long. He even had bat wings, a lion's tail with fur at the tip, and sharp nails that would rip your body in half. He was half human and half something else. Gray skin complexion, and a green eye in the middle of his forehead.

A cyclops?

Oh come on. What is this? Hercules the movie?

He had two black horns that were massive, and sharp. The demoniacal figure noticed I stopped in front of him, so he stopped too. He was just a few feet away from me, just close enough to do some damage. I felt his breath.

GROSS.

It was surely unpleasant. Probably leftovers from rotten bodies he had eaten years ago. All of a sudden, the beast crossed his arms across his muscular chest, and spoke to me.

"We finally meet, Ethasus!" he said with a hiss.

Even his tongue was snake-like, and his voice was deep, ogre deep.

"I've yearned for this day to come," he spoke again.

"Yup! I get that a lot. You must be another one of my fans, do I know you?"

"This is finally the day I get to skin you alive, and wear your flesh like a leather jacket," he snickered.

I was grossed out at the sound of that, and wasn't prepared for such an image in my head.

I started panicking. My body started trembling in fear again.

"Why aren't you running?" he asked, taunting me.

"Was I supposed to? I actually wanted to make this celebration a little more interesting," I replied, still grossed out and frightened.

"Oh?" he said.

I quickly got on one knee, and picked up a handful of dirt with my right hand. As I stood back up, I tossed it straight into his eye.

He cried.

While he tried to brush the dirt off, I saw an opening and I took it. I punched him in the back of his knee. When he lost his balance and leaned sideways, I kicked him in the stomach. The force knocked the air out of him, and he bent down on one knee. He was grunting and growling like an angry lion. He got on his feet quickly, and his wings spread wide open, as a defense mechanism. If I was any closer, he could've cut me in half. He had an angry grin, and was about to strike back, but I was ready for him. He flew at me, I rolled to my right and he missed. He turned around again, and with his sharp nails, started swinging. He used his wings to confuse me. When he swung his right wing, I dodged and used my arms as shield.

Yeah I know, bad idea.

He kept striking at me with his left claw, and got me square on the chest. I was bleeding.

It wasn't a big and deep wound, but it hurt. While I looked at my blood, he caught me off guard, and came at me again with force. I fell on the ground, hard, hurting my lower back.

OUCH!

He got on top of me, and with the back of his hand, slapped me square in the face. Why do they always go for the face?

I almost blacked out from that one. My head was spinning, and I was bleeding from my lower lip and nose. I tried to hold him back with both hands, but he was too strong.

I couldn't hold on. Left, then right, his teeth clacking over and over again, trying to rip out my jugular vein.

He was salivating, and his drool was falling on my shirt.

YUCK.

Once again, I could smell his revolting breath, close to my face.

I was getting tired.

I looked around and spotted a small rock. While still holding on with my left hand, I tried reaching out for it. I saw another demon making his way down from a hill.

OH NO.

They were going to gang up on me, I thought. The one eyed freak noticed I couldn't stand a chance with one hand, so he grabbed my arm, and drove my wrist to my side, then quickly grabbed the other, and did the same.

I couldn't move.

There was no way I was able to defend myself now.

I was a goner.

I was kicking and squirming, trying to get him off me, but it was futile. He was heavy and strong, and I was outmatched.

"There's no way someone so weak could have defeated Satu. I guess he'll thank me greatly, when I bring him your head," were his last words.

I stopped struggling, closed my eyes, and waited for the painful death. Fortunately for me, there was a loud roar. It came from the other demon. The beast looked up, and his expression turned to terror. He got off me, spread his wings, and flew away so quickly he left a cloud of dust enveloped around me. Some went into my lungs, and I started coughing hard. I couldn't even see the other demon now, but I heard him coming, and he was getting closer. I got on my feet, and ran so fast my thighs were burning. I ran into this rocky structure that had small gaps between the walls, and was big enough for me to fit in. I literally jumped inside and tried not to make a sound. Whatever scared the bejeezus out of Satan was now coming after me. The demon stopped in front of the big rock. I still was not able to see it, but I heard his steps. He was sniffing the air too. Something gently landed on my shoulder, which freaked me out.

I swore it was a bug.

Before I could realize it was just a feather, I had already stumbled over a few rocks, hit the back of my head, and blacked out.

DETARRU ISLAND

Dusk came fast for the Ross Family. They waited impatiently, and they were worried sick. Clara was finding it strange that there were still no Detarrunians around. She started questioning the security of the island.

"What's taking him so long?" Jack shouted, breaking the silence "It's been hours. You don't think he's—"

"For God sakes, Jack! No. He's not dead," Nathan assured.

"Then, why isn't he back? Tell me."

"I don't know."

He sounded just as worried as Erick's parents were. After all, it wasn't his intention to harm him. He just wanted to find Satu before Jack did, and take all the credit. He let his jealousy cloud his judgment, and for years, he'd been after Jack's research. He always wished that Erick, The Chosen One, could have been his own son. He hated that Jack had everything.

Even a beautiful wife like Clara. A Guardian of Detarru Island. His emotions got in the way, and because of his decision, he wasn't going to forgive himself if anything happened to Erick.

"Nathan, I swear, if anything happens to my son—"

"Oh please, Jack, cut the crap. Since when did you even care about your only son? You didn't even know who he was until a few hours ago. You're only worried because he's part of your damn research!" Nathan shouted.

Jack lost it.

He grabbed Nathan by his throat with both hands. He squeezed as tight as he could. Nathan was running out of air. He tried to get him off, but his grip was too tight. Everyone tried to pull him away, but they weren't strong enough for this mad man.

"I am going to kill you, Nathan. I swear I will!" Jack screamed with clinched teeth, while Nathan almost choked to death.

"Jack? Jaaack? Let him go!" Clara yelled, trying to calm him down. She placed her hand on his shoulder, and very calmly said: "It's okay. He's going to be fine. He is The Chosen One, remember? He'll find his way, in due time."

Jack seemed to relax after what she said, and let Nathan go. Nathan pulled away from his grip, coughing and trying to breathe again.

"Look. I'm sorry, Jack. This wasn't part of our plan. We didn't know Erick—"

"Reserve your apologies, Nathan," Clara shot back. She was angry too. Her son was stuck in the Underworld, all because of them. She also blamed herself for believing that giving birth to Ethasus, and raising him as her own child, would protect him from harm. Even protect him from his own father. She never thought that her secret would be revealed. She started crying again. She felt like she had failed Erick and his guardians. Jack saw her weeping, and went to console her. He knew how painful it was for her to know that Erick was dumped in hell, looking for a creature that probably might kill him. He thought if it weren't for this research, his son would've been safe in New York with his new friends. He shouldn't have brought his family here. Why was he so egotistic and only thought about his work when he had a beautiful perfect family to care for? Why didn't he listen to Clara, and her warnings? Why didn't she tell him the truth about Erick? If only he knew, he would've ceased searching for Satu a long time ago. Why keep searching, when the answer was his own son all along? How did he not see the obvious? It was weird for Jack to have Ethasus as a son, but his love for him grew a lot stronger. That moment he wished he were one of Erick's loyal guardians too.

Inferno

I regained consciousness and noticed I was in another world. All the pain, agony, and turmoil was gone. My body and soul were finally free, and there was no white noise. I don't remember what happened back there. All I remember was being chased by one of my tormentors, and then I blacked out. I remember falling, but everything went dark after that. Maybe I died in Inferno, and now I'm in another hell. Could there be multiple levels of hell? If so, then so help me God.

I can't take this anymore.

I've been in this black hole for too long. This place is changing me, and I'm not even sure if I'm the same Erick I used to be anymore. This place has made a lot of anger build up inside of me, and holding it inside isn't the best thing to do either, because now I've been tearing souls apart for a change. I learned to fight back as self-defense, but killed many trying to protect myself. My life will never be the same anymore. I guess that's what hell does to you. It takes over you, mentally, physically and emotionally, until it turns you into one of their own. Another loyal servant to Lucifer's cause.

I was lying on my back, and my body ached. I opened my eyes, and found it strange to see colors, and light. It wasn't bright, but it was very dim and enough to make my eyes hurt. All those years in pure darkness sure messes up your eyesight.

Strangely, I was able to see clear in the dark, back in Inferno. I guess it was a special ability you earned once you cross to the other side.

In this world however, I had to cover my eyes until they got adjusted to the light again. I turned to my side and rolled on my stomach, but my body felt very heavy and weak. I never ate while I was in Inferno, so I couldn't have been overweight.

Maybe it was the gravity.

I laid my head on the floor to recover my strength, and felt sand on my cheeks.

Was it sand? It can't be.

I forced myself to get on my knees, and when I did, I looked around. It was nothing but a red sky and a deserted world. The sand was red too, like blood.

"Hello?" I cried.

There was a hellish silence. I didn't see any spirits in this part of the world either.

What is this place?

I got on my feet, and I did my best to focus. I wasn't sure if hell had a North, South, East or West, but I had to choose which direction to go. I decided to walk straight ahead; maybe I'd find someone, maybe the same one-eyed demon that almost killed me back in Inferno. Besides, I wanted to get some retribution.

And so I started on a new journey in the red world.

CHAPTER 9

HOURS LATER

THERE WASN'T A SINGLE soul on this side of hell. The good part about the underworld was that I never got thirsty, hungry or sleepy. I did get tired a lot, since physically and emotionally you still felt pain.

I've been walking on Mars for quite some time now, but I keep stopping and resting during my excursion, which got me nowhere. I got freaked out when a thought came to my mind, the thought of being stuck in here for all eternity, alone and walking in circles forever. I got on my knees, and just stared ahead at nothing. I would've rather been in Inferno, punching demons, than on Clifford the big red planet. I was beginning to mope from frustration. I tried to think of home, but few memories came. The little flashes that came up in my head were short and blurry. They were memories of my parents.

Were they still alive? How many years has it been since I last seen them?

I put those memories away, since they weren't helping me at all. I couldn't linger in the past anymore, I had to move on. It was the only way of surviving in this reality. From the corner of my eye, I saw a creature on four legs moving towards me very slowly. It had black and brown fur, and glowing red eyes like fire. I stood up quickly, ready for an attack, but the thing just kept its distance, trying to read me or something.

It was studying me while it walked around in a circle. Then it stopped and sat.

What was it doing?

I saw how his tail between his legs waved back and forth like cats' do.

My body froze.

I couldn't believe my eyes! I've seen this animal before! It was the same German Shepherd that we brought to Detarru Island.

How is this possible? Can it really be? It had to be! That's the only dog I've ever seen with glowing red eyes. How could he have gone through The Gates of Hell? I thought I was the only one with that ability. Yet, there he was, right in front of me.

I took baby steps towards him, then extended my hand to pet him. I wanted to let him know I meant no harm. He just stared.

"Milo?" I called.

He cocked his head.

"You remember me!" the thing spoke.

I thought I was hallucinating. I think the big red planet had me going coocoo for coco puffs, and now, I was seeing and hearing things. If I were to guess, it looked like the dog had a smile on his face too.

"You're joking!" I said.

"What is there to joke about?" he asked with this British accent, which sounded like that one butler from Batman.

"You're not real. Get out of my head, demon!" I shouted, backing away from him.

"Demon? I'm no demon, child," he answered.

"Then tell me this, if you're so real, then how did you get here? Huh?" I asked, not convinced at all.

"Well, through The Gates of Hell, of course," he said flatly.

He was right though. There is no other simple way of putting it.

"Then, explain this awkward conversation we are having right now"

"That's because you're a weirdo," he mocked. "I think you've spent too much time here in Purgatory, and now you've lost your mind."

"This is Purgatory?" I asked in awe.

"That's right!"

"How did I get here?"

"I tried to get you in Inferno, but you ran off like a maniac, and ended up here, when you fell into a portal," was his answer.

"That was you? I thought you were another demon chasing after me. How did you know where to find me?"

"I'm a dog, remember? I can smell your stench from miles away."

Should I kick him now, or later?

"So, what you're saying is, you went to some networking events, connected with a bunch of demons, and now you've got VIP access to travel from one dimension to the other? How does a dog get to do that?"

"I don't follow " he replied in confusion.

"Never mind, fur ball. So what now? Are you here to rescue me? Or you're stuck in here too?"

"I came here to help you find your way back."

"Well, getting out is not going to be easy," I said. "There's demons everywhere trying to eat my guts out."

His smile disappeared and he came closer to me. This time he started sniffing my clothes.

"Hey, what are you doing?" I would've kicked him dead on the nose too, but thought he might bite back, so I didn't do it.

"My God! I was right!" he exclaimed. "It's only been a day and you've turned into a complete looney!"

I ignored that remark. The dog was a hell of a character. He sure was amusing.

"What do you mean a day? I've been trapped in here for years."

"Ah! Yes. For us, on Earth, it's only been a day. Time doesn't exist here in the underworld."

"Who are you?" I asked. I wanted to know how he was even

involved in all of this. How can this dog possibly know about the underworld?

He looked straight into my eyes. I noticed his 'I mean business' expression. I stood there silently, waiting for him to speak, while he stared back with those red glowing eyes.

"My real name is Matheus Lazores. I was given the task to watch over you and protect you."

"So, if your job is to watch over me, then that means you've watched me butt naked when I showered? Even when I took a dump?"

Even through his furry face, I saw he was annoyed. He gave me a stern look.

"I see the clown in you never changes."

"Which side are you on?" I asked again, still not trusting him.

"Neither," was his answer.

"So, why are you here? Are you here to help me? Or not?"

"I have something to show you," was his reply.

"You came all the way out here, just to show me something?"

"Correct!" he said, with a warm smile.

I almost giggled. This was the first time I've seen a dog smile.

"Come with me and I'll show you."

"Where are we going?"

"I can't tell you unless you see for yourself," he responded. He turned and started strolling ahead. I wasn't following. He turned to me again: "Well?" he said, "Are you coming?"

I didn't trust the dog, but if he had answers to all of this craziness, then I guess it was worth the try. Therefore, I joined him.

Together we strolled for another hour. So far, there was nothing to see but a red, sandy, and uncharted world.

Matheus stopped.

I stopped too, almost tripping over him.

Stupid Dog.

He stared ahead. I did too, but I couldn't figure out what we were staring at exactly.

"Wow! Look at that! I see a lot of nothing!"

He ignored my sarcasm.

"This is what you've been looking for," he said with a serious voice. I stared blankly at him. I was definitely not understanding.

I looked up, and didn't see anything. I started walking straight ahead. My adrenaline was rushing and I was nervous. Very, very nervous. One step at a time, I counted my steps. 1, 2, 3... I was going up a cliff, 46, 47, 48. As soon as I got to the edge of the small cliff, I saw it. There was a humongous crater in the middle of the desert. To me, it was shaped like an upside down pyramid. It wasn't deep, but it led downwards to something. I focused on an obstacle in the very bottom of the crater. Right in the middle, there was a square metal steel cage. It was about 10 feet tall and 36 inches wide.

I had to get closer.

I started going down to the bottom of the crater and it was very steep. Take a wrong step, and you'd be falling down-hill, and crack your head open. Matheus was right behind me. He wasn't having a hard time like I was. When I finally got to the cage, I tried to peek inside, but there weren't any holes or small windows. It was all steel. I didn't even see a lock, or chains to keep it shut. I studied the structure for a few seconds, both sides, back and front. I noticed it had a Detarrunian marking in the middle, the same skull-looking face that I saw on that skeleton key, which was used to unlock The Book of Mythos. I looked back at Matheus, who was also staring at the cage.

"In case you're wondering, this is an ancient burial chamber. This chamber was sealed with magic many centuries ago. This is where Satu was incarcerated, by you."

I had a flashback moment. The dream I had before coming to Detarru Island and the scratching sounds on a steel wall. Could this be connected?

The moment when you forget to breathe, and the whole world stops in front of you.

"Satu is inside that thing?" I stammered. I backed away slowly.

I didn't want to be anywhere near that monster. "Can he hear us? Is he alive?"

Matheus stared at me, entertained. He walked to the cage, and opened the door with his right paw.

"The chamber is empty," he announced.

"What?" I shouted. The hair on the back of my neck stood up. "Let's get the hell out of here, hurry!" I was about to run from fright.

"Get a grip. He's not in the underworld," he guaranteed. He looked like he was ready to smack me in the back of the head with his paw.

"Where is he?" I asked still a little shaky.

"This is what I wanted to show you," he kept on. "I wanted you to see for yourself, that before you and your crew came to the island, the Satunians prepared a surprise attack on the Detarrunians. They have slaughtered a huge percentage of them. Some of them were lucky to escape, but many were not as fortunate. Now that Satu is on the loose, he has already prepared his army to destroy mankind," he concluded.

"That explains a lot. That's why the island wasn't guarded as it should've been. Are they all dead?" I asked, worried.

"Most of them left the island."

"What about my parents? Are they…?"

"The Satunians have been preparing for their next attack. They are not aware that your parents are on the island yet."

"So the Satunians are really preparing for war?"

"Yes, and Satu might be considering going global this time."

"This is getting way out of hand, Matheus. All this time, I thought that beast was still locked up in here. I didn't know he was out there getting ready to do damage on Earth. We need to do something, what should we do?"

"Unfortunately, you are not strong enough, neither do you have the power required to complete the task."

"What task? What are you talking about?" I countered.

"You must understand; you aren't the Ethasus that you once

were before. You are weaker, and definitely not knowledgeable of the things from the past. Therefore, you won't be able to change this future."

"Look, there has to be something we can do here. Take me back to Earth, I'll tell my parents about Satu. Mom knows a lot about this guy, and she knows his weaknesses. I'm sure my parents will be able to figure this out."

"You're the only one who can figure this out. There is a way you'd be able to fulfill your destiny, and destroy Satu for good."

I eyeballed him up and down, waiting for an answer with anticipation. He was killing me with all the suspense.

"Come with me to Paradise," he said.

"Are you serious? You expect me to just walk up to Heaven, have a cup of tea with you and Zeus? I really don't have time for that right now," I said pointing up at the sky.

"Someone is expecting you. You won't stand a chance against Satu if you're not trained properly."

Here we go again.

"Just take me back to my parents. Together, we can figure something out. I know for sure my mother knows a way."

"I can't."

"Why the heck not?"

"Ethasus, listen to me. We need to go to Paradise."

"There's no reason to go there, the way out is back to Earth, so take me there," I demanded, infuriated. I really wanted to get out of this place, and he wasn't helping at all.

I think I ticked him off.

His glowing red eyes glared at me.

"And there it is again, the reason why you'll never be that courageous Ethasus you once were before. This is why Satu will reign once more, and you will not succeed. The world will crumble down in ruins, because their hero is a failure, hard headed, undisciplined, immature, doubtful and refuses to listen to simple instructions!" he shouted.

I couldn't believe he just said that.

My blood was boiling inside of me, and so far, I wasn't doing a good job with anger management in this place. I sure didn't appreciate this dog telling me what I can or cannot do. Especially calling me a failure, when all I've been trying to do is survive. Who does he think he is? Isn't it courage when you're pushed into hell, and tortured for days? Not to mention, when you have to erase all memories of the people you love. A sacrifice you have to be willing to make, in order to carry on with this destiny. One that I never chose. If that isn't courage, then what is?

"You think that by spying on me, you got me all figured out?" I shouted back. "Well you're wrong, you don't even know me. You have no idea who I am, or what I've been through. Yes, I might be irresponsible, hardheaded, undisciplined, immature and doubtful, but it's only fair, because I'm only human. How dare you judge me? How dare you call me a failure, when all I've been trying to do is not be a disappointment to all of you? At least I'm trying to help, and sort this mess out. So stop assuming that you know everything about me, because you most definitely do not!"

I looked straight into his eyes. He backed away slowly, with his tail between his legs, and ran off. I guess this was his way of defusing the situation.

I was still heated, pacing back and forth, mumbling angry words, trying to cool off.

2 minutes later, Matheus retuned and sat in front of me.

"What is it now?" I said.

"I was wrong, my apologies, Ethasus. I never thought such words would affect you in such a way. My intentions were only to make you see reason, but in the process, I did not choose my words carefully and upset you instead. You are absolutely right! I don't know you. I don't know what you've been through, and surely, I am no one to judge. The only thing I know is that you are the savior of the world, and I am your counselor. It is my duty to guide you on the right path, and to make sure you succeed, because if you fail, then I'll fail too. We all will."

I looked at him sideways and stood there quietly. He spoke with the honest truth. He was only trying to help me. I calmed down, thought about what he said, and had a flashback moment again. I remembered a time my mother told me that her duty was to protect me no matter what. I didn't understand back then what she meant, but now I did. I was chosen to destroy Satu, so I'm not as useless as I thought I was. If that's the case, whoever Bruce Almighty is up in heaven definitely won't turn his back on me.

"Which way is Paradise?" I asked.

CHAPTER 10

THE GROUND STARTED SHAKING. It had to be an earthquake, or a Purgatory quake.

Whatever.

"What is that?" I asked, trying to hold on.

The sand was moving, and there was sand falling down from the top of the crater. We were standing in the worst place for this quake. If we didn't move fast, we were going to end up buried under tons of sand.

Matheus' ears were upright. His posture was even different, and he wasn't relaxed any more. He was worried. There was something wrong.

"We must hurry! We can't stay here any longer, follow me!" he shouted. He ran off ahead.

He was running up the steep hill and I was right behind him. It was difficult to hold on, especially when you're running up a hill and the ground is moving under your feet. Even worse, the sand was falling in my eyes and mouth and it was hard to breathe or see.

"Hurry, Ethasus!" he screamed. "Hurry!"

I was trying my best to climb up, but the more I tried, the more I was sinking back down. We heard a sudden boom, like an explosion. It came from the bottom of the crater. I looked behind my shoulder and watched the ground spread apart, revealing a horrendous, dark chasm.

I never felt so terrified in my life.

I watched in horror as the ground disappeared under us.

"Ethasus?" Matheus called, trying to get me to focus. "Grab on to me. Don't you let go, you hear me?"

I grabbed on to his furry tail as he struggled to pull me up. I pushed down with my feet as hard as I could, since the ground was still moving. Together, we made it to the very top of the crater, but we couldn't stop there to catch our breaths. The sand was still sinking all around us.

"Come on."

We got away from the crater and the quick sands. When we got about 30 yards away, the ground stopped moving. We paused for a few seconds, and it felt like my lungs were going to blow up. I looked back at what used to be a crater shaped like a pyramid, now a vacuous void.

"Matheus? What's happening?" I cried. Matheus was scanning the area for a way out.

"Something's wrong. We really need to get you to Paradise, there's—" he didn't finish.

There was a loud roar. It came from the dark hole in the ground. Matheus' glowing red eyes locked on mine in terror.

"This is impossible," he said in a very low voice.

"What is it?" I asked persistently. I needed answers.

There was another roar and it was louder. We started running again. Whatever was coming out of that thing sounded big.

"This way, Ethasus. Don't stop, and don't look back," were his instructions. I didn't like it. The ground was shaking again and this time, it wasn't another quake. Something was coming out.

I was told not to look back, but curiosity was killing me. As we ran, I took a quick glimpse over my shoulder. My mouth dropped as a black cloud was forming.

That was not the scary part.

There were trillions and trillions of one-eyed demons flying side by side, forming a giant sand storm. They moved together in one motion. They must have forced their way out from one dimension to the other. By the way they were moving, it seemed they went through all that trouble just for one thing. They were heading this direction and fast. They were coming for us.

"There's no place to hide, we won't be able to get away!" I shouted as we ran.

The giant cloud was almost on us.

"Quick, get on my back!"

"Do what?"

In just a quick second, the dog transformed into another creature. He grew wings from his furry back, which stretched about 14 feet in length, and 36 inches wide. He had gold feathers, and two long ones on the crest of his head. His jaws turned into a peacock's beak, and his neck grew majestically long. I'd heard of this legendary creature before in ancient Greek mythology, but never thought I'd see one in real life.

He was a Phoenix.

"The King of Birds," I whispered. Then a thought came to my mind. Why didn't he turn into a bird when we were struggling to get out of the crater in the first place?

Stupid dog—err... bird.

"Ethasus?" he called. I quickly hopped onto his back. As soon as I held on to his long neck, he took off full throttle. I almost lost my grip when he swirled up in the sky vertically. He seemed to be going 300 miles an hour, and he was surely flying too fast for me to hold on to. For crying out loud, I never rode on a giant bird before, and big birds didn't have seat belts either. If I fell off, for sure I was going to be a nasty Humpy Dumpty. I was not prepared for this, and definitely not for what was coming up next. The swarm of cyclops was almost on us. One of them was right on top of me, and with his long claws, he started lurching at me. He almost got me on my back, but he missed. As he tried to strike at me again, Matheus swerved to the right, and sped up. Now the demon was right on Matheus' tail. He grabbed on to his feathery tail, and plucked a few feathers off his skin.

He cried in pain.

As retaliation, Matheus curved and spread his left wing wide. I turned to see what he was going to do. We slowed down a bit, causing the one-eyed demon to smash into his wing. That didn't knock him out though, but he sure was off our tail by a few seconds. We sped up again, descending to lower grounds. The further away from these beasts we were, the better. The demon recovered and was gaining on us again, while the black cloud made its way down too.

"How can we get rid of them?" I asked, looking back.

"We are going to have to fly through the portal," he replied. I didn't ask how, because whatever he had in mind was surely better than getting caught by those things. Three cyclops were on us then. I wished I had a weapon to fend them off.

SWELL.

I'd have to use my fist then.

The same demon from before tried to attack Matheus. He used his long fangs to bite on his neck, while the others were trying to charge at me.

"Hold on!" he shouted.

He got lower to the ground and did a 360. The demon still held on to his neck, but seconds later, slammed into an elevated cliff on the ground.

We only heard the PUFF Sound.

I was so distracted on the fallen demon that didn't realize one of them had me. He grabbed on to me from behind, and was trying to pull me off Matheus. This one wasn't very big in size, so he wasn't as strong. I tried to get him off by elbowing him in the chest, but that didn't work.

"Matheus!" I screamed. It was too late. By the time he realized, the beast had yanked me off his back and I was captured. The demon flew upwards, while still grasping on to me.

Matheus was coming back for me, full speed.

He banged into his head, and then we all splashed into the red sand. The demon was still holding on to my arms, and wouldn't let go. As a last resort, Matheus violently smashed his head with his beak, killing him instantly. His blood was purple, and it was such a sickening scene. I freed myself from the thing, but the swarm already surrounded us.

We were too late.

They formed a huge circle around us, but kept their distance. Matheus and I were back to back ready for an attack.

"Stay close to me, Ethasus."

I did just that.

One of the demons came forward, and spoke to us.

"Hand over the kid, and we'll let you go back to Paradise alive," he ordered.

That was the same green-eyed demon that almost killed me back in Inferno.

"On the contrary, Rukus, lay a finger on him, and you'll be going back to Inferno dead," he countered.

That was epic.

There was a lot of fuss coming from the crowd of hell after what he said.

"You fool, look around you, you're outnumbered. You can't take us all," Rukus affirmed.

He was right. There was no way we'd be able to take these guys on our own. I hoped Matheus had a Plan B.

"What is it you want with him?" he asked curiously

"Our orders were to bring him back to Inferno."

"By whom?"

"That is none of your business," he snarled.

"Well it is now, especially when you brought an army just to find one boy. Was that really necessary? Something tells me your superiors have something big in mind."

Rukus seemed to feel like Matheus knew too much, so he got really serious.

"Like I said, we were told to bring The Chosen One back to Inferno. This is none of your concern, so do not meddle with these territories."

"Well just like you, I have my own orders, which is to take him back to Paradise."

I felt like an object waiting to be sold to the highest bidder.

"So if you don't mind," Matheus continued, "I have an important delivery to make, as per his Excellency, Elios."

Rukus' eye went wide open. Everyone started talking amongst each other again.

"Unless of course, you want me to call him down here for confirmation," Matheus kept on.

Rukus stared awkwardly at both of us. He wasn't very happy with the intel, or the threat for that matter. He had no choice though, so he turned to his demons, and motioned them to retreat. He glanced at Matheus one last time.

"Satu won't be happy about this, and rest assured, there will be a war between dimensions. Once it does, I will be coming back for you, and I will have your head on a stick," Rukus exclaimed with a cynical growl.

YIKES!

Whatever dispute these two had against each other, I sure didn't want any part of it. Matheus kept his posture, and he didn't look intimidated, or at least, he was trying not to. The swarm blasted off, and flew back to wherever they came from, including Rukus, who was still glancing back at Matheus with a demoniacal glare.

That was creepy.

"What was that all about?" I faltered.

Matheus didn't answer me.

"Just a minute ago they tried to kill us, now they just flew off because of an Elios? Who the heck is Elios?" I asked perplexed.

"There are barriers between dimensions, Ethasus. On Earth, you have a system in America, which is called the check and balance of power, and without it, there is no government. We have a similar system here too. This one is called The Order, and it stabilizes good and evil. A war in the underworld would not only be decided amongst God and Satan, but by billions of other gods and devils just like them."

"Wait, hold on a second, this is way too cosmically for me.

Can you rephrase that? In human language?" I said, going out of my mind.

"What I'm saying is, there are other devils and many other gods. Many of those are a lot more powerful and destructive than the ones we know. If a war is started between these powers, it will be the end of everything as you know it. An Endless Ending."

GULP.

That sounded ominous, especially the part where both worlds will cease to exist. I mean, we believe that when we die on Earth, we go to heaven or something, but if we die in heaven, where do we go then? My head was hurting. I was giving all this too much thought. For Christ sake, it's not like I'd ever thought of these things to be an actual possibility.

"So what's Satu's role in all of this?" I asked with desperation.

"Think of him as a threat. Even though his intentions might not be to unbalance the equilibrium of The Order, he's still using unnecessary force to eradicate the mortal world as we speak."

"So in other words, he is more like an underworld terrorist?"

"Exactly right. If Earth is destroyed, that will also be catastrophic for this world too."

"You mean Purgatory?" I asked, bewildered.

"Yes! This world is a mirror of the other. Purgatory separates Inferno from Paradise, or Good from Evil. If Purgatory is destroyed, Paradise and Inferno will collide. The Order will be broken, and the battle between dimensions will begin. Something tells me that someone else, other than Satu, is behind all of this. We really need to get to Paradise."

PARADISE

Since I was a child, my father has taken me on many different ventures. I've been to places, explored things, and seen so much beautiful artwork from all around the world. That was nothing compared to this. I never imagined such a world existed. It was astounding, and I couldn't believe that I was there in the flesh. We flew through a sphere of white light that was hidden in a cloud in Purgatory. As soon as we flew inside, the ring of light closed behind us. That must have been another underworld portal. We were flying over a tropical cabana blue ocean.

Yes! An ocean.

No more, red uncharted wastelands. Even the skies were ocean blue, and very bright. The world was colorful, and there were many more suns, I counted about 20. There was a fresh spring breeze, the air was pure and clean, and it was just perfect. As we descended, I saw land in the distance, and it was green, just like on Earth. The mountains were beautiful and humongous. I even saw chunks of land floating still in the air. Each of these individual floating lands had different cities. These cities had skyscrapers so high, they almost touched the sky. Paradise was an enormous and ultra-majestic city. Instead of houses, there were castles or manors. They were also big, and they were all made out of blue crystals. Even the bridges were made out of glass. It was the most beautiful thing I'd ever seen in my life. The whole world was like an orchestral song.

It was sweet, it was good, it was right.

Matheus landed right in front of a fortress, which was the main entry to the city or the cities. I was anxious, and I wanted to see what type of spirits lived here and what they looked like. As soon as we got closer to the giant wooden doors, we heard a roaring sound. They started opening by themselves, as if we were expected.

We walked inside, and there they were.

The Paradise spirits.

They all stared back at me quietly. There was a huge crowd at the center of the city, where they waited for us to arrive. All eyes were on me and Matheus, which made me a little uncomfortable. They looked like regular people too, just like on Earth. There were all kinds of spirits, all races, but their physique was so perfect, so filled with joy, happiness and love. They were beautiful people. All of them wore white shirts and pants with sandals. I was surprised to see children, and they looked happy to see me too.

It was an incredible feeling.

They all stared in reverence as Matheus and I walked through the crowd. They each parted, making way for us, as we headed from one city to the next. A female spirit came running towards me, and she hugged me tightly. Tears came down when she let go.

"I'm so glad you're here," she said with a sly smile and in this sweet vocal sound. She kept walking and disappeared through the crowd.

"Why was she crying?" I asked Matheus.

"Because you give them hope. They believe in you," was his answer.

I was thoughtful for a second there.

Matheus and I came across this house at the very top of a hill, away from the city. It was different than the rest, and was built in an earthly fashion.

I stared at the city again.

Every corner I looked at was filled with wonders.

"Welcome to Paradise!" Matheus said with a warm smile. He was still a Phoenix, and it was awkward to see a smiling bird, but I wasn't surprised.

"This place is incredible," I said.

"It is! This is just one part of Paradise, from many more."

"You mean, there's more Heavens?" I asked, dazed.

"Oh no, my dear boy, this is not Heaven."

"It's not?"

"Heaven is a holy and sacred world. No one is allowed there."

"Then what's in Heaven?"

"The gods," was his simple reply. "And the creator of 'The Six Realms."

"The Six Realms?"

"Yes, they are Earth, Inferno, Purgatory, Paradise, Hell and Heaven," he explained.

"So, if Paradise isn't Heaven, then Inferno isn't Hell," I concluded.

"That's right."

"What about devils?"

"They've been exiled to Hell by The Creator. They've been trapped in there for 1,000 eons. However, that hasn't stopped them from doing evil on Earth. They have their demons to do the dirty work for them and they are all around us. Anyone could be easily manipulated to turn into a devil's ally."

"Just like Satu?"

"Exactly! He wasn't always evil you know. One day he was tempted into trading souls to the devil for immortality. The more he killed, the more powerful and heartless he became."

Matheus started walking again, towards the house. He walked right in, or squeezed in. I was right behind him.

"Why don't you just turn back into a dog again?" I asked.

"Believe me, I wish I could, but I can only transform once per dimension. I haven't quite mastered that ability."

"You haven't transformed in Paradise though."

"I know," he said with a smile. "But you will be needing me to fly you back to Earth again later."

OH.

The inside of the house wasn't that welcoming.

There wasn't any furniture or picture frames and it was just a big round hall with white marble floors. At the end of the round hall, there were double stairways, which led up to the second floor. We went up the stairs, and came across an old man with gray hair, whose back was facing us. He was on his balcony, looking out at the city. He was wearing a white long sleeve shirt, white pants, and sandals.

"Ethasus is here, just as you requested," Matheus announced.

Who was this guy anyway?

My question was answered as soon as he turned to face me, and my heart stopped. This was definitely unexpected.

"Hello, Erick," he said with a warm welcoming smile.

His voice brought back memories.

Oh how I missed that voice.

I didn't respond, because I was still dazed. It took me a few minutes to compute what was happening.

"Oh my! You got bigger."

It was him in the flesh, right before me. I thought I was never going to see him again, yet, there he was. I walked up to him slowly, wanting to confirm he was real.

"What's the matter, Dumbo? You look like you've seen a ghost," he said, joking. When I was a little boy, I used to have big ears, so he called me Dumbo. That only confirmed that he was 100% real.

I hugged him, and he hugged back. I wished that moment could have lasted an eternity. Seeing my grandfather again was magical. What was happening was simply impossible, but there he was, in the flesh, and this moment was real. I'd been lost in the underworld for who knows how long, but when I hugged my grandfather, I felt home again.

"Am I dreaming?" I asked, letting go, trying to avoid a major disappointment.

"Can a dream do this?" He pinched my arm hard.

"Ouch!" I cried.

He laughed, then I laughed too, then we both laughed hysterically for another minute. It was just like old times.

"It took you long enough. I've been waiting here for so long I grew gray hair, look," he said, playfully touching his hair. "There's a lot of things I've been dying to tell you."

"Word, me too! Did you know about my secret identity?"

"Are you kidding? I knew about you since the moment you were in your mother's womb," he replied.

"How did you know?

"Because once upon a time, I was one of your first guardians on Detarru Island," he chuckled.

"No way!"

"Yes way! In fact, I was right by your side when you defeated

Satu and his army for the first time. Together we succeeded, and I know we will do it again."

"I don't know, Pops. How am I supposed to do this? I am much weaker than before. I'm basically useless," I said disappointed.

"That doesn't mean you're useless. That only means it isn't your time yet. Trust me, you'll know when you're ready, and when you are, you will succeed."

Listening to him brought back memories again. I remembered those days where out of nowhere, he would give me a pep talk and say these exact words:

'No matter what happens, never give up.'

I wondered if he was preparing me for this moment.

"What are you doing in Paradise?"

"Waiting for you," he replied. "This is where we always meet."

"What do you mean?"

He looked at Matheus, who was standing behind me quietly.

"So you don't remember anything about your past?" he asked.

I shook my head.

"That's really strange. I thought by now you'd remember something." He crossed his arms across his chest and thought for a moment.

"Well then, I guess I'll just have to explain everything." He smiled. He took a deep breath and continued.

"First you must know, this won't be your first or last time here in Paradise. Satu is not the only one who's been threating the world. Many have tried to destroy Earth before, and they'll keep trying. When they do, this is where we meet, and find The Others."

"The Others?"

"Just like you, there are other valiant men and women, chosen to protect Earth!" he exclaimed. It was kind of relieving to know that I wasn't the only Power Ranger alive, but something just didn't add up.

"So why aren't these Others doing something about Satu?" I asked.

"Because just like you, it isn't their time yet," he answered. I got quiet for a minute, and tried to compute all of that. My grandfather sat on the floor, so I did too.

"Not their time yet either, huh? So then, where are these other Mutants?"

"How would I know?" he answered with a shrug.

"You don't know?"

"I said I was one of your guardians, not a psychic, Dumbo," he replied.

"Do you at least know who they are?"

"Nope," he replied, shaking his head. "You secretly choose them yourself."

I could not believe it. This was a matter of life and death. I really needed to build my own Justice League, or I was definitely going to end up dead.

"It's alright," he continued. "Once you're ready, you'll know who The Others are, and what to do."

"How will I know when I'm ready?"

My grandfather looked at me, then at Matheus, and nodded. Matheus smiled kindly, came forward, and handed me a pair of white pants, and a white shirt, identical to what my grandfather was wearing. Then he said, "First, you need to get yourself cleaned up. Harris and I will show you around Paradise, then teach you all you need to know in due time."

I was responsible for the wellbeing of six realms. One of them is Earth. If I didn't do this right, The Clash of the Titans would begin, and it would be game over for all of us. I couldn't help it.

I was afraid I'd fail.

CHAP+ER II

DETARRU ISLAND

"Do not let anyone in or out," ordered a man with a black long cape and a very soft crude voice. His hoodie covered his face, creating a dark shadow.

The Satunian soldier bowed, then ordered seven of his men to follow. They jogged to the small entryway that led downwards to a cave.

"My Lord?" came a voice from behind a building. It was Oliver, the messenger. He was some kind of witch or visionary with telekinetic abilities, and was able to communicate with spirits or demons in the underworld. Short for his age, late fifties, he was dark skinned and very skinny, with shoulder length white hair and perfect teeth.

"I have words from the underworld," he said. "The Chosen One has made it to Paradise."

The man in the cape turned, furious. "Who was in command?"

"Rukus, sir," Oliver answered with fear.

The man in the cape clenched his teeth, and with an irritable gesture said, "I want Ethasus and his guardians dead, do you understand?" he snarled.

Oliver nodded.

"Where are The Others?"

"We, we don't know their whereabouts yet, my Lord. We are doing everything we can to find them."

"When you do, bring them to me, alive," he said, with a grin.

"As you wish," Oliver said.

"Is everyone in position?" he said, as he was scoping out the Detarrunian village.

"Yes, we are waiting for your orders, sir."

"Good, we will strike tomorrow morning."

Oliver bowed before him, and made his way back into the building. The mysterious man took off his hoodie, revealing a shiny bald head. He was in his late sixties, tall with menacing silver eyes. His arms and legs were muscular, and he had scars on his face and body from previous battles.

He had his entire army on a mission, to search and destroy. All he cared about was power, and he wanted to wipe out humanity from existence. Creating his own demonic realm on Earth was something he'd been trying to do for centuries. As he stood there, he felt the presence of a guardian.

"Let go of me!" screamed a woman being dragged out of the cave by two guards. She was thin and elegant, with hazel eyes and brunette curly long hair. Right behind her was a man whose hair had shades of gray, and he had brown eyes that hid behind his glasses. Seconds later, an average man with blue eyes, red hair and a beard was dragged out, followed by a blonde woman with gray eyes, and a muscular guy that took three soldiers to restrain. They were all squirming and yelling, trying to get loose.

"My Lord? We found these men and women hiding by the gates," the guard in command said.

"Clara?" the man in the cape spoke. He leaned closer, and got a better look at her. She didn't reply, and just stared at the tall man with scars, who was also staring back at her with a malicious glare. Seeing him back again, had her trembling in fear.

"How did you get out? Where is my son?" she screamed. "Where is Erick, you bastard?"

He backed away slowly. He didn't know what she was talking about. "Who's Erick?"

"Don't play dumb with me, you monster; he went to Inferno looking for you. What did you do to him?"

His eyes were still fixed on her for a moment. Then he finally realized who she was referring to.

"AH! You mean Ethasus?" he asked with a grin. "He's your son?" He chuckled. "I haven't seen him, unfortunately. In case you haven't heard, there's a price for his head, and every demon in the underworld is searching for him now. So as far as I'm concerned, he's probably already dead," he scorned softly.

Clara didn't say anything after his wicked response. She stood there quietly, thinking.

"Satu?" The blonde lady with gray eyes called. He glanced at her with this intensity. He sure didn't like servants addressing him by his name, and didn't like being interrupted either.

"I'm Rebecca Taylor and this is my partner, Nathan Jeff," she said. "We were the ones who freed you, and lured Ethasus into The Gates of Hell, with this book."

She handed him The Book of Mythos. He took it, studying it for a moment.

"I don't recall ever asking you to speak," he finally said, almost in a whisper.

Both Rebecca and Nathan exchanged looks, puzzled. A guard slapped her across her face, hard. She lost her balance and fell to the ground. Nathan helped her up while she wiped the blood from her nose.

"This book is worthless to me, and so are you."

Rebecca stood there in silence, rubbing her face in confusion. She thought that Satu would reward her greatly for her actions, but it didn't seem that way anymore. She betrayed the guardians and joined the Satunians for nothing. He was probably going to kill her as a sign of gratitude. She made the mistake of dragging Erick into the underworld, and now he can't come back and save them.

They were on their own now.

"Where are The Others?" Satu asked, looking at Clara.

"I don't know what you're talking about."

Satu lost his cool. She could see his jaw movements from where she was standing. No one expected his sudden reaction either. It was so fast that he looked invisible for a quick second. The only thing Clara felt was his big cold and rough hand on her throat. He was so strong that with just one hand, he lifted the woman up in the air.

He was choking her for answers.

"If you know what's good for you, you'll tell me where they are," he said with clenched teeth.

Clara was running out of air. The more she fought, the more he held tighter.

"Let her go!" the man with glasses yelled.

Satu quickly turned to him. The other guards held him down.

"And you are?" Satu asked, interested.

"I'm Jack Ross, Ethasus' father, and that's my wife, so get your hands off of her!" he demanded, with no signs of fear.

Satu watched him perplexed for a moment, then gurgled.

"Is this what the new generation of guardians are doing? Mingling with the outsiders?"

He let Clara go, and she started rubbing her throat in pain. He definitely left a mark on her. His focus now was on Jack. He took a few steps, ready to attack him.

"Wait!" Clara shouted, knowing his intentions. His attention was back to her again.

"You don't understand, there is no way we could possibly know that. Only Ethasus knows who they are, and where to find them."

Satu's expression turned to anger. That piece of information turned him wild with rage and he screamed like a wild animal. He grabbed Gregory by his collar, and threw him up in the air, so high he landed on top of a rock a few feet away, dead. He ordered his guard to deliver a message to Oliver. When the guard in charge walked away, Satu turned back to Clara and Jack.

"What are you going to do to us?" she asked.

He stopped and took a deep breath, and just like that, his anger was gone again.

"There has been a slight change of plans. I'm going to have to let you go."

That was an unexpected answer.

Clara and Jack were not convinced. They didn't know whether to believe him or just run for their lives.

"You're just gonna let us go?" Rebecca asked. She sure broke the awkward silence.

Satu ignored her and walked away. He ordered his guards to let them go, then they all went inside the building, leaving them in the dark.

Clara and Jack didn't waste any time. They ran back to the terminal, and didn't care if Rebecca and Nathan followed or not.

They were on a mission.

"I really don't buy it!" Jack exclaimed, while running.

"Me neither, but Satu is getting his army ready. Therefore, he won't touch Erick until he finds The Others first."

"That's great news," Jack said relieved.

"I just don't know why The Others are so important to him."

"Who are these Others?" he asked, eager to know.

Jack's research had escalated into another level that he could no longer understand. Now everything was a fictitious reality. He realized there was more to this island's legend than he expected. The only way of finding answers was through Clara.

"The Others are Erick's most trusted allies," she informed him. "Just like the guardians, they were also chosen. Yet they are much more powerful than Erick himself. Their purpose is to help Erick when The Order is at risk."

"The Order?" he said bewildered.

"Yes, it is a law created to balance good from evil in the underworld. As long as that balance of power exists, there will be peace in all six realms."

"What if they are destroyed?"

"It will be the end of everything," Clara responded.

Jack stopped running. He was thoughtful and concerned.

"Are you saying that our son will be in the middle of a major battle? And if he doesn't win, it will be the end as we know it?"

Clara nodded.

"Clara? He's only 16 years old. How can he possibly save all the worlds?"

"I know exactly how you feel, Jack. Luckily for us, we have a backup plan in case things get out of hand."

"What's the plan?" he asked.

"I'll show you once we get back to New York, but we need to hurry! I think I know where Erick is, and if I'm correct, he should be safe with my father in Paradise."

"Harris!?" Jack glanced at her, shocked.

Nathan and Rebecca were heard catching up to them.

Jack was ready to fight them again, but Clara held him back.

"This is not their fault and neither is it ours," she said softly. "I gave birth to Erick, thinking he could have a normal life, and be a normal kid. I thought I could protect him, and change his destiny. Unfortunately, he was destined to go through those gates no matter what. We cannot control that."

Jack stood there silently, listening as she kept hitting him with facts that were too hard to understand. To him, it was very unfair to know that his only son was trapped in the underworld, and was destined to fight demons for the sake of mankind.

"Jack? Wait up please," Nathan called out behind them. Jack and Clara waited for both of them to catch up.

"I'm so sorry, please, let us help you bring Erick back," Nathan implored. "We made a mistake and we want to—"

"You're only sorry because you got ditched, and your dumb plan didn't work out," Jack said annoyed.

"Let's keep moving," Clara interrupted.

They finally got to the truck, and they headed back to the terminal. Clara went on about the Six Realms, and her father, Harris Montclair, the very first guardian on Detarru Island.

She went on about other things that Jack needed to know, like The Others, and The Creator. This side of the story he had never heard of before, in any of his research. Neither had Nathan and Rebecca. They never thought such things could even be real. There were more secrets about Erick that Jack never thought were possible. Now he knew why she never told anyone.

It was for Erick's protection, and the protection of the world itself. He started to accept it. He finally realized how valuable and important his son really was. Even in all that anguish and desperation he was feeling inside for not being able to help him, he was still one proud parent.

"Will he come back?" was Jack's response to everything Clara told him.

Clara looked at him and smiled warmly and she gently grabbed his hand. "Of course he will."

PARADISE

"That does it?" I shouted in frustration. "For Christ sakes, Pops, I'm going to be fighting demons, not teddy bears." My grandfather and Matheus just listened while I complained, in silence. I was about to go Super Saiyan in a minute if they didn't train me the right way.

"Well what did you expect, kiddo?" Pops said.

"I thought you were going to teach me some Harry Potter moves, or how to give Satu a punch to the throat. How is learning about the past going to help me with anything?" I said annoyed.

"With that negative attitude, you won't understand what I'm trying to show you, Erick," he responded calmly.

"What exactly do you need me to see?"

"I need you to see within yourself"

"Look within my wha?"

"Look inside of you, feel your soul, your energy, and find that heroic spirit that you once were before. Let him guide you once more."

"How?"

"First I need you to close your eyes, and take a deep breath."

I did exactly that. "Okay, now what?" I asked.

"Now relax, and keep breathing in and out."

"I am relaxed."

"No you're not."

"Pops, I did exactly what you said, and I'm relaxed," I said, not relaxed.

"Okay, now, I need you to try to clear your mind."

"Okay I did."

"This is a very important process; if not done right, it won't work," he advised.

"I swear I'm not even thinking how dumb this is. I've cleared my mind, trust me," I said, being negative.

"Now, listen to your soul, and tell me, what is it saying?"

"Umm…"

"Can you hear your soul?" he asked.

I took few seconds to respond. "No. I can't hear anything."

"Well, that's because your mind won't allow it, you must believe."

"Pops? This is not working," I said, even more aggravated.

"If you would just shut your mouth for one second, and stop thinking stupid things, you might hear a thing or two," he said, sounding irritated.

He was killing me.

I stood up, and just stared at the city from frustration. He was right though, I needed to relax, but how could I be relaxed? I had a huge responsibility on my shoulder.

"I don't get it," I said, feeling down and disappointed "Why was I chosen? I can't even fight, so what's so great about me?"

"Why do you think so little of yourself, Erick?" he said while he stood right next to me. One thing I loved about my grandfather was that he always listened. He knew when to ask the right questions, and most importantly, he always had the right answers.

"Because I'm always afraid. How can I possibly save the world, if all I do is live in fear? I feel like this was a mistake, and I'm going to fail you guys," I replied, saddened.

"To be afraid does not mean you will fail." My grandfather spoke kindly while smiling. "It means you're not perfect. It means you make mistakes, just like everyone else does. Fear is a normal and common human emotion that we cannot control. It is a way to overcome what we cannot understand. It is a way to test our strengths, from our weaknesses and in some cases, a way to challenge ourselves to be better. I believe to learn from our mistakes is to be courageous. You don't need to know how to fight to win battles. The Creator didn't choose you to be tough or intimidating. He chose you simply because of who you are."

I let those words sink in.

"Promise yourself something, Erick," he continued. "Promise yourself, that no matter how scared, lost, discouraged, or even hopeless you might find yourself, you'll never give up."

"How can I promise that? I'm useless, I'm not like The Others," I said, discouraged.

"Because, unlike The Others, you have the greatest heart, and the mightiest soul. That alone is the most powerful weapon you could ever use, against Satu or any demon."

When he said those words, I felt something inside of me and I felt energized. Those words really went straight to my heart and spirit.

That's because he was right. I couldn't live in fear all my life, I had to be more positive, I had to start believing in myself, and my guardians. So, I made myself that promise, that no matter what happens, I was never going to give up.

"Thanks for understanding," I said, feeling better.

"Don't thank me, this is what I'm here for."

"So, should we start over?" I asked with a smile.

"Of course!" We both sat down again. I started with the

breathing, then relaxing, and then clearing my mind and listening to my soul. Unknowingly, I went into a deep, meditative state of mind. There was a powerful rush of energy flowing through my body the whole time. An image of Earth popped up in my mind.

Earth! It had been a long time since I'd seen that world. I wonder what's happening out there. Was it the futuristic world we've all seen on TV? Had my parents gone back to New York safely? Had Satu conquered the whole world already? Did Kate Anderson ever get married?

Matheus told me it's only been a day since I walked through those gates. Time doesn't really exist in the underworld, so I'm guessing everything was still normal back there. If I was lucky enough, I could still make it to the football game and show Mike my awesome skills.

"Holy crap!" I shouted, opening my eyes.

I remembered everything, even something Larry had told me before I had gone on that trip the day before.

I remembered it clearly!

It was like a film being played over and over, right before my eyes. It was the answer I was searching for.

'When you're finally ready, come find me... We'll get The Others.'

Matheus and my grandpa both smiled at each other. They knew this was supposed to happen.

"You're almost ready!" Pops said. "Let's go!"

Detarru Island

"Ethasus is back," Oliver informed.

Satu was quietly standing by the gates like he was expecting someone. He turned to Oliver, and gently nodded.

"Good! Are my men ready?"

"Yes, my Lord."

"Have my army commence an attack in the city at once. I want everything destroyed," Satu ordered.

Oliver obediently went to gather his army, while Satu, with a wicked plan in mind, walked through The Gates of Hell, and disappeared into the underworld.

CHAPTER 12

Earth

"RUN TO THIRD, PATRICK, run!" Larry screamed at Patrick from the benches.

Bruce, Larry, Patrick, Luis and Jimmy were all at the school playing a game against Mike's team.

"I'm running, I'm running!" Patrick shouted back, as he ran to third base. It was a bit difficult for him, since he was a little overweight. As he ran, he kept looking back, making sure he knew where the ball was. One of Mike's players in left field dropped the ball, which made this his chance to score.

"Don't stop, keep going!" Jimmy instructed.

Patrick ran as fast as he could.

He made it to third, but kept running to home. Left field player quickly threw the ball to Mike, who was pitching. Mike saw Patrick was halfway to scoring, so he ran after him. He was only inches away when Mike picked him up and slammed him on the ground, hard.

Patrick looked dead after that one.

"Touchdown! Woohoo! Hehe!" Mike screamed victoriously. The rest of his team were enjoying and celebrating that too.

"Mike, this isn't football, idiot!" Jimmy screamed at him.

Mike didn't really care.

"Patricio! Dale un trompon al cara de fuiche ese." Luis also said, in his Dominican slang.

"What?!" Patrick finally was showing signs of life.

"I said, punch him back!" Luis translated.

"Okay," he replied while still lying on the ground, not moving. He thought all of his bones were crushed.

Bruce came over and helped him up.

"Are you okay, man?"

"No," Patrick replied.

"I told you guys, this game is for sissies, I want to play a real game," Mike said with boredom.

"Yeah, well me too. I can't wait till Erick beats you this Friday," Larry countered with a smirk on his face.

"Me neither," came a voice from behind the fence.

Everyone looked back in awe.

"Maybe he'll shut you up already," the stranger said, sitting on the bench. Everyone stepped back horrified.

"What is up with you nerds? You're acting like you've never seen a girl before."

They kept staring at her, as if she was some kind of goddess.

"What are you doing here?" Larry asked.

"What do you think? I'm here to watch you lose. Do you have a problem?"

"Ah, yeah? Your face is the problem," Larry argued.

"Chill Larry, that's no way to treat such beauty," Mike interrupted.

"Fine, I'll leave, but I'm telling Mom that you've been skipping summer school," she responded mischievously. One thing she was good at was being very manipulative of her brother.

"Of course you can stay, Kate. I didn't mean what I said, I was only kidding," he lied, with a fake smile.

"Much better," she said satisfied.

"So? Sexy lady!" Mike continued, barging in the conversation. "How's my honey bun doing?"

Kate glanced at Mike in disgust. "Actually, I've changed my

mind." She started walking back home, but Mike grabbed her arm.

"Stay a little while, I'm about to start a real game with my boys."

"Get lost, Mike."

"You're hurting my feelings."

"Mike! I said buzz off!" She shoved him aside.

"Oh come on, baby, don't be like that," he begged.

"I'm not your baby, and you're pathetic," she said displeased, while walking ahead of him. He stopped for a bit, realizing how true that was. Yet it was still Kate, the hottest girl in school.

He didn't care.

"Kate?! Wait for me!" He ran after her, trying to catch up.

"Dude, Mike is way too obsessed with your sister. Aren't you going to say something?" Luis said, walking up to Larry, who was getting his football gear ready.

"Nope, no need," Larry replied, calmly and not bothered.

"Jesus, Kate, why would you do that for?" Mike grunted in pain. Kate had kicked him between his legs, hardcore. As Kate walked away, he came back to the field slowly, and sat by the bleachers, still rubbing his privates.

"I just love the sound of karma," Patrick said, pleased.

Mike didn't respond. He was in way too much in pain to even bother.

"Alright! Who's ready for a new game?" Jimmy asked amused.

Home

It was good to be back!

Earth was so different compared to Paradise. There was something different about being here though, and it was strange. I felt alive again, felt really thirsty and strangely hungry all of a sudden. So much that I was about to faint.

Welcome back.

"I thought the only way out was through Inferno," I supposed, holding on to Matheus while he flew over my neighborhood.

"Good heavens, Dumbo, that would've been catastrophic," my grandfather said, also holding on next to me.

"Why?"

"Someone gave the order to have us killed. I was told that every demon is searching for you down there, for a high price. I know this was Satu's doing, for sure."

GULP.

The sun was out, and the sky was clear. What a beautiful day to be back. We landed right in front of my house. The area was clear, and there were no neighbors around. Matheus took advantage of the opportunity, and transformed himself back into the German Shepherd he used to be.

How cool was that?

I stood in front of my house, and just stared at it in wonder. It looked so different. I was away for so long in the underworld, I didn't recognize my own home anymore. I was about to walk up to my porch when I accidentally bumped into someone. I was so distracted with the house, I forgot to watch where I was going.

"Hey! Watch where you're going, jerk!" the girl said, agitated.

When I turned to apologize, my stomach shrunk. I felt a sting all over my body. The girl had a hot pink t-shirt on, with white shorts and white sneakers. She had beautiful long brown hair in a ponytail, and a curvaceous perfect body. She gave me a mean glare with those amazing blue eyes of hers.

I just couldn't believe it. It was Kate Anderson!

"I'm sorry, I—I didn't see you there, are you okay?" I said, trying to recover.

She didn't respond, and just stared me down. Her eyes were so intimidating, she had me looking away a few times. When I looked down for a moment, I finally understood why she was staring at me like a pile of poop. For starters, I had sandals on, with high water pants, and a white shirt made out of some celestial material.

Way to go, Erick! Definitely a great way to impress, dork.

"Umm, hi! I'm Erick. I moved here a few days ago," I stammered, extending my hand. She took it, but didn't introduce herself. I already knew who she was either way.

"It's nice to meet you. Do you live around here?" I asked, still trying to make conversation. She nodded, finally, but I was feeling a little awkward.

Was she anti-social? Or maybe she hated me for even talking to her with sandals on.

"You're the new kid everyone is talking about? Right?" she said at last.

People were talking about me? I hope it wasn't in a bad way, and I sure hope it wasn't about my secret identity.

"They are? What are people saying?" I asked, a little worried.

"That you're playing against Mike on Friday. I totally want to see that!"

"Oh! Well, I guess that's me," I said, not so thrilled.

"Don't worry, I'll be cheering for ya!" she said smiling, patting me on the back.

"I'm glad!" I responded, with a shrug, smiling back.

"I'm Kate," she finally introduced herself. "I live next door to you."

My heart stopped. Did she just say next door to me? She pointed at the white house, next to mine.

"You live there?" I asked, confused.

"Yeah, why? Is that surprising?" She lifted an eyebrow.

That was so sexy.

"Oh, nothing, it's just that, I thought my friend lived there. I guess he must have moved out or something," I said scratching the back of my head, still puzzled.

"You mean Larry?" she asked, while rolling her eyes.

I nodded.

"That's my older brother."

"Wow! Really? He forgot to mention he had such a beautiful little sister," I said playfully, but man, how I meant it.

"Thank you," she said smiling.

She was perfect!

Cough, cough.

I heard someone clear their throat. I looked behind me, and it was my grandfather and Matheus watching how I made a fool of myself. I totally forgot they were even there.

"Umm, Kate! This is my grandfather, and this is Mathe—umm, dog, er—Milo," I faltered. They both waved at her.

"Hello," she said waving back. "Hehe, your dog is so cute. He waved at me!"

"He what?"

"He waved at me. That was pretty cool." I looked at Matheus, who winked at me smiling.

That idiot! Can he be any more obvious?

"Oh! Yeah, he's one of a kind, isn't he?" I said, with a phony smile "You should see him do other tricks, like climbing up trees and things."

"Your dog climbs trees?" she said with an odd smile.

I think Matheus knew where I was going with this. I winked back at him, smiling mischievously. I could tell he was ready to bite my head off, but he kept it cool.

I was enjoying myself.

"Here Milo, here boy!" I mocked. "Come here, buddy"

Surprisingly, he did come to me. I asked him to sit, and he obediently sat too.

Kate was impressed.

"Who's a good boy? Now, show Kate how you climb a tree," I said. He never tried to climb the tree like I expected though. Instead, he lifted his hind leg, and started peeing on me. I felt the warm liquid running down my feet and sandals.

EWW GROSS!

I was really going to kill that dog. As I kicked him away, I heard my grandfather laughing behind us.

"Well, he sure owned you," Kate mocked, while laughing hysterically. She had the most beautiful smile, which kept me staring, and I couldn't help it.

What a beauty.

She made me forget about Matheus and had me smiling too. Matheus sat right next to Kate, and she gently rubbed his head.

I noticed his grin.

"Why are his eyes red?" she asked. I really didn't have an answer to that, so I decided to get some retribution.

"Uh, he's umm… sick."

"Sick?" she said, with this facial expression of disgust. She slowly took her hand off him.

"Yeah, he's got pink eye. It's highly contagious."

Matheus wasn't enjoying this one.

"But, his eyes, they're glowing—" she exclaimed, still wondering.

"Yeah, the uh… animal eye-drops, they really have some epic side effects."

"You are quite a funny guy," she said, giggling.

"I try."

"Well, I gotta go now, umm, it was nice meeting you, Erick."

"Same here, Kate, uh, see you around," I said, still staring at her as she walked away.

She was about to walk inside the house when she stopped for a moment, to take one last peek at me then went inside.

"Did you guys see that?" I said excited. "She looked back at me!"

"So what, that doesn't mean anything," Matheus responded.

"Maybe for you," I said. "Besides, you're just hating because I'm a ladies' man."

"Absolutely!" my grandfather broke in. "My good looks do run in the family!"

"Oh God, here we go again," Matheus said, rolling his eyes, not wanting to hear it.

"You see, I remember back in my day—"

"Uh, Pops?"

"Yeah?"

"I'm sure you were a gorgeous supermodel then, but can we save the world first?"

"Oh, right."

Mom had placed a spare key under a flowerpot. I got the key and unlocked the door, and we all went inside. The house was empty. I guess my parents were still stuck on the island. I ran straight into the kitchen fridge, and made myself a gigantic ham and cheese sandwich.

That was really good.

I felt like I hadn't eaten in days. I also felt so thirsty, I almost drank a whole gallon of water. After my meal, I headed upstairs, changed into regular clothes, then went downstairs to meet up with Pops and Matheus who were outside, discussing our next plan.

Something was wrong.

Earth started to tremble underneath us.

"What was that?" I asked. We all ran down on Sunnyside Street, and saw the neighbors trying to find out what was happening too.

There was an explosion, followed by screams. A nearby building just exploded in pieces. Another explosion was heard, then another nearby.

We were being attacked.

I saw Kate running out of her house, and she looked scared. She saw me standing in the middle of the street, and ran towards me.

"What's happening?" she shouted.

"I don't know."

Another explosion blew up a car nearby, and a few people got hurt. I ran over to help them, but they were injured really badly. There was an older guy who had severe burns on his arms and legs, and there was a young woman lying unconscious on the ground. Together, Kate and I dragged them away from the burning vehicle. Other neighbors tried to help by treating their wounds.

"I need to find my brother," Kate said.

"Where is he?"

"At the school."

There were more screams and police sirens heard. There were also ambulances and fire trucks on every corner of Sunnyside Street.

This was really bad.

"Let's hurry," I said to everyone.

We started running and when we hit the intersection, a gigantic fireball hit the front of my school. The impact was so strong, it knocked all of us off our feet, and we landed on our backs. I glanced at the building, and it was on fire. I got up quickly, and helped Kate and my grandfather. We started running again, and got to the baseball field, which was empty.

"Are you sure he was here?" I asked.

"Yes, I was just here 30 minutes ago," she replied.

Another fireball hit the field, followed by an explosion. Thankfully, we weren't close, but it could've injured us. More screams were heard coming from the neighborhood. I looked over to my left, and there were houses on fire, and some were crumbling down. I saw people running like crazy in the distance. I looked up at the sky to see where those fireballs were coming from, but I didn't see anything.

"He couldn't have—?" Matheus mumbled.

"He couldn't have what? Who?" I asked. Kate gazed numbly at both of us. She couldn't believe my dog just spoke.

"Ethasus? We need to find The Others now," Matheus kept on.

There was a monstrous scream.

We all looked around, but didn't see anything. All I heard was wings flapping. Whatever it was, it was heading towards us. I looked up at the sky again, and there it was.

A giant cyclops.

How? Did these things follow me here?

He came on to us, and we dodged him. He made a 360 up in the air, and came back for another round.

"What the hell is that?" Kate screamed, terrified.

I watched the demon, perplexed, who had crossed over to my side of the world.

"Looks like Satu has opened another gate here on Earth, and released his demons," Pops said.

"He did what?" I shouted.

This monster wasn't the only one attacking us. There were hundreds, chasing the neighbors and hurting them. The demon flew at us again, and almost got Kate.

Oh no he didn't.

I grabbed her by her waist, wrapped my arms around her, and pulled her away from danger. I wasn't going to let anything happen to my future girlfriend, no sir. The demon missed Kate, but then turned to me.

"Look out!" my grandfather warned.

The beast almost got me this time, but I ducked before he could cut my head off.

That was close.

"How can we get him off our tail?" I asked.

"Cyclops have a weakness. It's their eyes," he informed me.

"What is that thing?" Kate broke in.

I glanced at her and I struggled to explain, but my head went blank.

"It's a long story. You wouldn't believe me if I told you."

"Well this is a pretty good reason to start?"

She did have a point. It isn't like you see demons every day, trying to attack humans, and fireballs falling from the sky. Not to mention, a talking dog.

"We need to move, now!" Pops shouted.

The demon landed. It wanted to attack us from the ground, or more likely, me. The thing stalked me everywhere. I scanned the area for something to defend myself with, and I saw the third base near me. I ran to it, and the demon ran after me.

I sledded towards the base on the ground, grabbed it, and bashed him, full force, on his face. The demon whined in pain.

He was bleeding from his jaw and upper lip. I think I broke a few teeth out of him too.

"Quick! His eye, Ethasus, his eye!" Matheus reminded me.

I quickly whacked him in the eye with one of the tips of the base, and his eye erupted with purple goo.

It was sickening.

He went tumbling down to the ground, dead.

Another demon spotted us. This was a different demon. I had never seen this one before. It was curvy on the hips and chest, had long legs, human feet and hands, with long black sharp nails. Body was slim and athletic, with long black wings, a long tail and its brown skin was lizard rough. Both its eyes were yellow like a snake. The hair was black, long and braided. The teeth were sharp as well. What made it even more terrifying is that the demon was female. In Inferno, I learned that all female demons were more dominant and more dangerous than males. We were all in danger, and we couldn't hide and we couldn't run.

The demon's eyes were locked on mine. She just observed my every move. She was squatting down, close to the ground, studying me like a cat, ready to strike.

My knees were trembling from fear and I thought I was going to get sick to my stomach.

"Come on! You want a piece of this? Come and get this, you scrawny, little—" I placed my hand over Kate's mouth as fast as I could. I sure didn't expect Kate to be suicidal. I had to shut her up, for all our sakes. Kate didn't like that, so she bit my hand.

Ouch.

"Interesting world," the demon finally said. "Never thought I'd see it with my own eyes." She looked around, intrigued.

"Who are you? And who sent you?" my grandfather asked.

"I was sent for him," was her response, still looking away, while pointing at me.

Yikes!

I was dying from fright as she stalked me again on all fours, trying to get closer to me.

I kept moving away.

"Though I'm very curious as to why Satu would need all my demons, to get one little boy?" she said.

Kate glanced at me, as if I was some kind of alien. All of this was pretty weird to her, so when she stared at me, I only shrugged and smiled. Kate wasn't smiling back, though. The demon stood up straight, and walked towards me.

Her hips swiveled from side to side, while her arms swung loosely back and forth, like a model. Matheus wasn't sure of her intentions, so he quickly jumped in front of me and acted as a shield. His glowing red eyes were fixed on hers. He growled at her, and unexpectedly, she did too, but her growls were louder.

"Out of my way!" she hissed.

"Go! Get out of here!" Matheus commanded.

My grandfather got the message and without wasting any time, he pulled Kate and me away from danger.

"Wait! We can't just leave him!" I shouted.

"We need to find The Others now, before it's too late," my grandfather responded.

"But she'll kill him!"

He kept trying to pull me away, but I kept pulling back. The demon and Matheus started fighting each other to the death. He would bite into her legs and arms and she would brush him off. She was too strong for him. He tried to jump on her several times, but she would punch him away or grab him, and slam him into the wall. I thought for sure he had crushed bones. Slowly, he tried to get on his feet, but she clamped her nails into his furry skin and picked him up with one hand. She was going to go for the kill. I refused to let anyone get hurt trying to protect me.

I pulled away from my grandfather and ran towards the demon. Her back was facing me, so she didn't see me coming.

"Erick! No!" my grandfather cried.

I picked her up with my shoulder and tried to slam her to the ground, but she jumped up and flew over my head, landing behind me. I turned quickly, swung, and I missed. I swung again, but she kept dodging all my punches. Her agility was unbelievable, and I knew she was toying with me.

Matheus jumped on her back and bit her shoulder. She delivered a powerful punch to both our chests; we were tossed away in the air, and we landed somewhere near the bleachers.

I'm not going to lie, that hurt pretty badly.

I couldn't move, and I also couldn't breathe. I thought I had dislocated a shoulder. The pain made it hard to catch my breath again. I looked over my shoulder, and Matheus was in pretty bad shape too. My grandfather came running, and tried to help me up.

"Are you okay?"

"Yeah, I think so," I said, trying not to worry him.

"Good!" He hit me in the back of my head.

"What was that for?" I asked, confused.

"What are you trying to do? Give me a heart attack?" he shouted. "Stop being a hero, or you're going to get yourself killed, Dumbo!"

I noticed Kate ran off somewhere, and I knew it was because she was horrified. Wherever she ran off to, I hoped it was a lot safer.

For some weird reason, I had this gut feeling that I just had to protect her.

"Kate?" I called.

She didn't stop. "Pops, go after her, keep her safe," I implored.

"But Erick?"

"Pops, please, do this for me. You said to listen to my soul, and that's exactly what I'm doing right now. Don't let anything happen to her," I said, while looking straight into his eyes. My grandfather looked at me for a moment, then he ran off after her.

"Ethasus, you need to get out of here!" Matheus yelled, hurt, while trying to get back on his paws.

There was another explosion, and it was closer to the school. It was another fireball. I hoped Kate and Pops didn't get hurt.

The demon got back to business. She picked me up, then

slapped me so hard with the back of her hand that my body twisted. I thought she broke my neck.

As I bled from my nose, I wiped it off with my good arm, then jabbed her in the jaw with my fist.

That didn't hurt her, but it sure hurt me. My knuckles were burning. As I rubbed my hands, she kicked me with the toe of her foot, right on my chin. I wasn't expecting that.

She then round kicked me on the side of my head, and I fell to the ground. I think I lost my sense of hearing, and I saw stars. Definitely was about to black out.

Matheus jumped on her back again, and with his sharp teeth, he bit her hips.

She screamed. I know that had to hurt.

She grabbed him by his fur and pulled him off her skin, and as she did, black blood was dripping from her back. That only made her more furious. She kicked Matheus to the ground with such force that he left a dent in the ground. She flew off up in the air, and stood on top of the fence. With the little energy I had left, I crawled to Matheus, who was on the ground, bleeding and hurt.

"Matheus?"

"Ethasus? Why are you still here?" He was weak and taking short breaths from the pain.

"I can't let you have all the fun!" I replied, with a bloody smile. "We can do this together."

He couldn't comprehend why I was so calm and confident. That gave him strength. He smiled back and nodded.

The demon was ready to attack again. She came back, full force, straight for us. Surprisingly, Matheus transformed into that majestic Phoenix I once saw before. With his huge beak, he caught her in the air, and tried to swallow her whole.

She refused to be bird food.

With her strong arms, she opened his beak and flew away. Matheus was faster, and pecked her on the head and she went down, moaning in pain. Her screams were horrible. So bad it hurt my ears.

Matheus was ready to charge again but her tail stretched out like a sharp knife, and stabbed him in his chest. He was severely injured.

"Nooo!" I screamed.

I ran to her and grabbed her in a bear hug. I saw her yellow demon eyes as she glared at me sideways. She pulled her tail from Matheus' chest. Then she slowly ducked, did a split, and I lost my balance. With her arms, she pushed me over her head and I landed on my back. She immediately stood up and placed her foot on my neck, and I was choking. Her focus was back to Matheus, who was regaining consciousness.

"This is between you and me, so leave him alone!" I said, gasping for air. I had her attention again. She could've broken my neck if she wanted to. Thankfully she didn't. Something tells me she wanted to torture me to death instead. She was now hovering over me with a sinister face, and stomped me right on my chest. It was the most excruciating pain ever.

"You're a tough one! I can see why your soul is worth a lot in the underworld." She stomped on my chest once more. I thought she broke a rib or two that time. "You are not like most spirits. You are very different. I love different. You could be quite useful to me," she sneered.

My body was in so much pain, I didn't even feel a thing anymore. I don't even remember what happened after that. All I could remember was Matheus calling my name, but his voice was fading away. Then everything went dark.

I blacked out again.

CHAPTER 13

I SLOWLY OPENED MY eyes.

Everything was still blurry and I felt lightheaded, and a lot of pain. The sun was still out, and I could still hear the chaos out on the streets. As I regained consciousness, I felt someone's warmth. I turned my head slowly and I saw these beautiful blue eyes staring down at me.

It was a familiar face.

I was laying on her lap, while she tended my wounds. Her perfume was strong but sweet and it smelled like bubble gum.

"Kate?" I said, surprised to see her. I was going to get up but she pulled me back down.

"Shhh, don't try to get up," she warned me.

I finally remembered the demon, and our deadly fight. I turned my head, trying to find Matheus.

Gladly, he was okay and he was sitting right next to me. He was back to his original form.

"Matheus!"

"Glad you're okay, Ethasus!" he said, happy to see me. I noticed his injuries were gone too.

"Where is she?"

"Where is who?" Kate asked, looking around.

"The demon," I responded, while I tried to sit up. I felt severe pain on my chest.

"She's not around anymore and we can't stay here. We might

get spotted again," Matheus advised. "By the way, that was a very brave thing you did back there, Ethasus. You stood up for me," he said respectfully.

"Nah! It was nothing."

"How did you do it?" he asked, eager to know. I sure didn't know what he was talking about.

"Do what?"

"You made me stronger, and I was able to transform more than once in this dimension. I just don't understand why you would put yourself at risk for me. It's crucial that you stay alive."

I took a moment to think.

"I just did what I thought in my heart was the right thing to do. You were trying to protect me, so I wanted to do the same for you. I felt the need to give up everything in order to change things. Besides, I was chosen to destroy Satu right? So The Creator wasn't going to let me lose to one lousy demon."

"I'm really glad you have started to believe in yourself, Ethasus," he said proudly.

Kate looked at me differently. I made her seem to wander off deep in her thoughts too.

"Where's Pops?"

"I'm right here, Dumbo" he answered. I looked over my shoulder and saw that he was okay and he also had a big smile on his face.

I realized why.

Right next to him were five other guys. I recognized their faces and I sure was happy to see them. I couldn't believe it was them all along. They were the ones I was looking for.

Jimmy, Bruce, Patrick, Luis, and of course Larry.

My allies, my friends, The Others.

"'Sup, Chief?" Larry said while helping me up.

"Hey guys!" I responded cheerfully.

"How did you guys find us?" I asked.

"We were playing a game, then we heard explosions and

people screaming. When we were on our way home, we saw these things flying around and hurting people," Jimmy started.

"Yeah, then we came across Harris and Kate who told us you were in danger," Bruce broke in. "We came running to kick some butt."

"Is she dead?" I asked.

"You mean the demon?" Larry asked.

I nodded.

"She flew off somewhere before we got here. I don't know where to," Larry replied.

"We have to get out of here," Pops said. My grandfather stopped in front of us and turned to face us all.

"As you all may know, from now on, you will not be able to go back to your families until this is all over."

"What?" Kate shouted.

"These demons know who you are now, and we cannot afford to lose any of you."

"But—I have to go back. My parents are in danger," she said panicking.

"Kate listen, Mom and Dad are okay. They called a few minutes ago."

"Where are they?"

"I don't know," Larry responded.

"None of us know where our parents are," Bruce added.

Kate was trembling. I knew she was scared and worried. I slowly walked towards her and grabbed her hand gently, and spoke calmly and firmly.

"I know that you think this might be a crazy nightmare, and that you'll wake up and it'll be over soon but this is all real, Kate. Your brother, Larry, my grandfather, the boys, we were all chosen to stop a demon, that if not stopped soon, it will be the end of the world. Not just this world, other worlds too."

She looked at Larry for confirmation. "You guys are really going to save the world?" she asked in disbelief.

She thought we were joking, but we were all serious.

"There's a lot of things that you need to know, but you must come with us and we can explain," I said.

She took a few seconds to let all that sink in. She looked up at Larry again, then at me. She nodded and accepted to come.

While we were walking down the intersection at Sunnyside Street, I had this gut feeling again. I asked everyone to make a right turn on Irving Avenue, which would lead us to the I-495 Interstate, towards downtown Manhattan. Surprisingly, Matheus and my grandfather were letting me lead the way.

They trusted me.

Irving Avenue was looking a lot more ruined than Sunnyside Street.

Cars were crushed, houses were destroyed, and some were on fire. We came across an unoccupied school bus that was parked on someone's front lawn. Fortunately for us, it was still running.

We heard screams and some growls. A few demons were heading our way.

"Hurry!" I shouted. "Get in!"

Everyone ran to the bus, while I was struggling to keep up. Thank goodness Patrick noticed and gave me a hand.

"Come on, buddy!" he said while helping me out.

As we were about to get in the bus, a lady came out of a house screaming and shouting for help. She had a demon right behind her. He grabbed her by her long hair and pulled back, then let go, causing her to fall on the ground, face first. She was hurt pretty bad. I couldn't bear to watch, I had to save her.

I ran to her.

"Erick? What are you doing?" Patrick shouted trying to stop me. The pain in my chest and body had me limping, but I wasn't going to let that poor lady die.

Luckily, Luis and Jimmy joined me and ran past me. They both attacked the demon in unison.

He didn't see it coming.

Luis grabbed him by his horns, while Jimmy kicked him right in the eye so hard, it exploded. Just like that, the demon dropped dead. Karma really got him good, and he sure deserved it. Yet I never thought these guys had so much strength in them. It was like nothing I'd ever seen before.

Luis fixed his hair and winked at me as I watched them in awe.

"Hehe, quien es el Matatan? Po yo!" he said in Spanish, cocky as usual.

My Spanish was not very good, but I think he said something like 'Who's the man? Me of course!' or something.

Jimmy helped the lady up. She was bleeding from her forehead and knees from the fall. She was in her late fifties, gray hair, very skinny, pale and fragile for her age.

"Are you okay?" I asked.

"Yes, thank you, thank you so much for saving me." She thanked us all, then she hugged Luis and Jimmy.

"You live alone?" I asked.

"I do, yes."

"Please come with us," I pleaded.

She hesitated a little. "Where are you headed?"

"To the city," I replied.

"Oh my, haven't you heard the news? It's dangerous down there. Everyone is evacuating."

"I know, and it looks like it's going to get worse soon. Listen, I would hate to leave you behind, so why don't you stick with us."

"Alright." She nodded.

We all ran back to the bus where the rest were waiting.

"Why are we going to the city, Erick?" Larry asked.

"There's something I need to do. Can you drive this thing?"

"Totally."

He got in front of the wheel and turned the bus around. We drove down the interstate. As I stood in the front of the bus, the guys were seated looking out their windows for any demons. The lady also sat quietly while cleaning off the blood on her knees with the tip of her skirt. I looked out through my window and saw that there were many abandoned vehicles on the road.

It was a mess.

It's like Satu wanted to wipe out an entire civilization.

We had to zigzag through traffic and drive in the emergency lane on the right. I noticed a few pedestrians running around on the streets. I guess they were running from demons.

"What is your name?" I asked the lady.

"Sarah. What's yours?"

"My name is Erick." I extended my hand.

"Nice to meet you, Erick." She took my hand.

"The old guy over there is my grandfather and these are my friends," I said, pointing at the guys and Kate. I mentioned everybody's name. "I hope you don't mind coming with us."

"No, not at all. Thank goodness you were around to save me. Do you know what those things are?"

I glanced at Pops and Matheus. I wasn't sure what to tell her. Pops joined the conversation and explained everything. She gasped, and couldn't believe those monsters were really demons from hell.

"No worries, Sarah, these guys will protect us," Kate said smiling.

Have I ever mentioned how gorgeous she was? I looked at her while she spoke to Sarah. The way she spoke, the way she smiled, then looked at me, then at Sarah. It was breathtaking.

They were having a conversation for a moment, and I think they were even talking about me, but I was too distracted looking at Kate.

"I gotta say, he's one of a kind, right, Erick?" Kate asked.

"Huh?" was my reply.

"Are you alright?"

"Uh, yeah! Yeah, I'm fine," I said, feeling like an idiot again.

"Are you two... you know? Going out?" Sarah asked.

"Umm, no, uh not exactly," I replied blushing while Kate shook her head.

"Hmm, well just so you know, you'd make such a cute couple," she suggested giggling.

At this point, Kate and I were feeling kind of awkward.

Kate spoke first. "Thanks, Sarah." She smiled, then turned to me. "Umm, we need to place some ice on those cheeks. They're looking really bad." She started touching my face.

"Ouch, that hurts."

"Sorry," she said with puppy eyes.

I forgave her MILLION times.

She walked to the back of the bus, looking for a first aid kit. When she found it, she grabbed the kit, then took out an ice pack, a few gauze pads and alcohol pads. She provided a few bandages for Sarah too. Then she started cleaning up my bruises and boo boos. Her hands were soft and gentle; I didn't feel a thing.

"You are pretty good at this," I said, admiring her.

"Really? Thanks! It comes with practice, I guess. I've always wanted to be a doctor."

"You should totally go for it!" I encouraged, smiling. She smiled back and continued cleaning up my wounds.

"I wanted to thank you," I said, breaking the silence.

"For what?"

"If it wasn't for you, I would've never found them," I said looking at the guys. She turned to them as well. She sat across from Sarah and started helping her with her wounds.

"Now I see why my brother respects you so much."

"He does?"

"My brother wasn't always like this, you know. He used to be such a jerk, and very rebellious for some reason. He was just always so…"

"Grumpy?" I finished.

"Yes! Exactly. Then ever since he met you, he changed drastically. I didn't understand why at first, but now I do. They all respect you and look up to you as a leader. You have a great heart, and that is very contagious. Because of that, they believe in you and now I do too!"

I was speechless.

"Look out!" Matheus warned.

There was a loud boom. Larry turned the wheels to the right, and we almost fell on top of each other. "Brace yourselves, we're being attacked!" Larry screamed.

I walked to the front of the bus and saw a few fireballs aimed our way from the sky. We dodged one of them, but the other hit the roof of the bus. It got us by an inch.

We were lucky. There were more fireballs seen from a distance heading our way.

"Larry, we need to get on the service road, now," I instructed. I figured we were a bright yellow cheese bus, for everyone to see. I thought maybe by driving on the service road, we'd have a better chance of staying unnoticed. It worked for a few minutes, then two huge demons spotted us again.

These two were different, and they weren't cyclops. They were uglier and bigger. No teeth, hollow eyes and no nose. Taller than an electric pole with long arms, and white skinny pale skin. One of them opened his mouth wide and a small fireball was created and grew bigger and bigger by the second.

So that's where they were coming from.

As soon as the giant ball got big enough, the demon spit it out, up in the air. Unfortunately for us, we were the targets. Larry again turned the wheels and dodged both the monster and the fireball. The turn was so unexpected; I didn't get the chance to hold on. I fell on top of Matheus and almost killed the poor thing. Sarah and Kate were holding on to each other while the guys watched in horror through their windows.

Both monsters ran after us.

"Faster, Larry!" Jimmy yelled. "They're gaining on us!"

"I am going faster," Larry countered, pressing on the gas. I took a quick glimpse at the speedometer and we were going 100 miles an hour.

Fast, but not fast enough to get away from these anorexic giants. One of the white devils stretched his long arms and smashed our back windows.

"Larry!" Kate shouted again.

"I know. I know!" Larry screamed at her. He was under a lot of pressure and his forehead was sweating.

"We need to get off on this exit!" I said.

"Where are we going?" he asked, concerned.

"I need to find an old friend."

Deep inside I was hoping this person had made it back to the city. If not, it was all for nothing.

One of the white devils lurched at us again with his huge hand. He missed, but made the bus swerve a little. We almost hit an abandoned police car. The other beast was about to launch another one of those fireballs but I saw the Midtown Tunnel coming up ahead.

YES!

The tunnel was too small for the beasts to follow. That was good news.

As soon as the demon launched the fireball, Larry hit the gas even harder. When we made our way inside, the ball hit the top of the tunnel, causing a big chunk of wall and rubble to come down on us. The impact was so big that Patrick and Bruce were lucky not to get crushed in the back. Luckily, the bus was still halfway inside, and we were able to get out.

"Everyone alright?" I exclaimed, making sure no one was hurt. Everyone was accounted for.

I checked on Pops and Sarah, both were alright. Then I made sure Kate was okay. Larry pulled the handle to open the door. Matheus was the first one to get off the bus and scoped the area for more danger.

Suddenly, a hand crashed through the back of the bus and grabbed on to my leg. It was so fast I didn't have time to react.

It was one of the white devils again.

I was trying to get free but the thing had a pretty good grip on my leg. He was dragging me out of the tunnel. Jimmy, Luis and Patrick all grabbed on to me and tried to pull me out of his grip.

It wasn't working.

Matheus came running fast. He bit the monster with his sharp teeth a few times. We heard loud cries and the demon was in pain, but he still didn't let go of my leg. Kate ran to the back and picked up a sharp piece of glass from the broken windows. She punctured the thing several times, then she stabbed the pinky finger, twisted the glass, pulled the skin hard, and then ripped it off, just like that. Red blood spilled all over her and my legs. I was baffled.

Not only was she HOT, but she could also kick butt!

After a few agonizing screams, the demon let go of my leg. He tried to pull the bus out, with us still inside.

Talk about stubborn.

Bruce helped me up and we all ran out just in time before the demon managed to get the bus out. The rest of the wall collapsed behind us and there was no way in or out from that side of the tunnel.

We were all gasping for air.

"Everyone alright?" Jimmy asked.

"That was close," Bruce said, still breathing hard. I looked at Kate who was trenched in demon blood next to me. She didn't look very happy.

"You totally rocked back there!" I said, even more in love with her than ever.

"Don't mention it."

She felt sick and had her arms out, trying not to touch the blood on her.

"We have to be careful," Matheus spoke. "Let's try to stick together. Danger waits in every corner. Let's get out of this tunnel before those things come back."

It was going to be a long way out.

CHAPTER 14

Manhattan

FROM A BRIGHT SUNNY and clear blue sky to a dark cold and gray ominous one, the city was looking more chaotic by the minute. More and more people were injured and more demons were destroying everything in their paths. Downtown Manhattan was no longer a city. Trains and subways weren't running and abandoned. Bridges were collapsing, and buildings were evacuated. 42nd Street and Broadway was no longer a street of attraction either. The big monitors were all shut down and some were broken. The few that were still functional were broadcasting the destruction of the city from helicopters. There had to be hundreds of white devils all over the city, blowing up buildings and streets with their deadly fire balls.

The Metropolitan Museum of Art was strangely the only building that had not been touched yet. Everyone had evacuated the city except for one specific group of people. There were hundreds of men and women lined up in front of the museum. They were all suited up in black and they were all armed.

The Satunians.

Their army expanded from 86th Street all the way down to 58th, between Lexington and 5th Avenue. That was only 1% of such magnitude of an army. There were thousands of demons waiting by The Gates of Hell. Waiting for orders from a bald man in a cape, standing in front of the Museum.

Satu.

He was looking at his powerful army while they looked back at their leader. Satu kept looking at the city's destruction. He enjoyed every minute of it. He erupted with laughter, celebrating his successes so far.

He raised his right hand and pointed towards the city.

Such command had the Satunian army, marching together towards their commanding posts.

"Lola?" Satu called.

A female demon walked up to him. It was the same female demon that wounded both Erick and Matheus.

"You called?" she said, standing next to him.

"Where have you been?" he asked furiously.

"Oh, just toying with humans!" she replied with enthusiasm.

"I need you to do one last thing for me."

"That'll cost you"

"I know." He forged a smile.

"Great! What do you need?"

"Your demons haven't found Ethasus yet. I'm starting to believe they aren't qualified for this task."

"Do not underestimate them, Satu. That will change once they start feeding on human souls."

"So why haven't you given the order?" he asked, even more aggravated.

"Because you didn't ask," she responded innocently.

Satu really disliked her.

"Find Ethasus, and bring him to me as soon as you can. Can you do that? Or is it too much to ask?" he said with gritted teeth. His soulless eyes stared down at Lola with a strong fortitude.

She found that very captivating in fact. She knew Satu was going to find every way possible to not lose this fight. He had a massive army now and the possibility of Ethasus winning this fight was very low. Nonetheless, he insisted in capturing Ethasus, which was very unusual to her.

"You must be desperate," she mocked.

He didn't like the remark. He stared her down again with that insensitive glare. Lola was never intimidated though. She ignored his cold stares and walked right past him. Her back was now facing him and she simply did not care.

He was surely a joke to her.

"Why do you need me to find him so badly?"

"It isn't your place to question me," he countered.

"Sure it is, because without me, you wouldn't have an army," she said flatly. Satu didn't reply. He imagined crushing her bones in pieces, yet he knew she was right. Lola was the Master Chief of Inferno, and she knew all the prominent demons. Even devils from other dimensions. He knew she was way too resourceful, but not for long. He had bigger plans in mind. One where his reward was going to be mightier than ever before. He only needed a source of power, one that he could control. He had the perfect group in mind.

The Others.

"You are absolutely right," he finally said, pretending to be nice. "The reason why I need your help is simply because if I have Ethasus, The Others will come here looking for him."

"What makes you so sure they'll come here just to save him?"

"Because they're buddies!" he said with a cynical laughter.

"Alright then, I'll do it, but like I said, this is going to cost you," she reminded.

"Of course! Name your price."

"Ethasus!"

Satu's eyes opened wider than a football. For a second he kind of wondered if she was referring to his soul, or did she have something else in mind?

"First tell me, what do you need him for?" he questioned.

"Not until you tell me why you need The Others."

Both were silent now. They both had big plans, none of which they would speak of.

When it came down to demons, it was 'trust no one,' or 'finder's keepers' types of ideals.

"Very well then, I'll hand you Ethasus once I have The Others," he bargained.

"It is always a pleasure doing business with you." She jumped up in the air, spread her black wings, and flew off over the billions of Satunians who were still marching off to their respective destinations.

Downtown

We finally made it out of the tunnel safely.

As we moved down the street, we saw a wave of people marching by. They were all in different groups, each heading different directions. They were all armed and ready. Men and women of all ages were marching together.

"Stay down," Jimmy warned. We all did as we were told and hid behind a yellow taxicab that was in the middle of the street.

"Who are these people?" I asked mystified

"They are Satunians," Matheus answered.

"What are they doing here?"

"Remember when I said Satu was gathering his army?" Matheus explained.

"Yeah."

"Well, this is just a small portion of them. We are not even counting his whole army of demons."

"This will happen nationwide if we don't stop them soon," my grandfather concluded with his voice cracking.

I couldn't think straight anymore and I was starting to feel anxious.

"Wait, so, Erick and my brother have to fight against that?" Kate asked, pointing at the crowd of people.

"No," was Matheus' answer.

"So then, why are we here?"

"We are here because we need to protect The Order and help Ethasus defeat Satu."

"How are we supposed to do that?" She was asking every question on the book.

I felt a lot better having her question them, instead of me. I was a walking question mark myself. The guys were just listening quietly next to Sarah.

"We have a backup plan," Pops announced. "I believe Christine arranged everything accordingly, even way before Erick was born. If things go as we planned, we will succeed!"

"Grandma is in this too?" I asked perplexed.

He nodded.

"What is the plan?" Jimmy asked.

"There you are," a rough, cold voice interrupted.

My heart was in my throat. It was the green-eyed demon, Rukus, from Inferno again. He had a few cyclops behind him too, ready to kill me or skin me alive just as he promised.

They flew after us.

"Run!" I shouted. Everyone scattered. Pops ran, holding Sarah by the arm while Kate also followed behind him. Matheus and I ran the opposite direction and the guys were right behind me too. Fortunately, the demons didn't go after my grandfather, Kate or Sarah, but they sure were on my tail. We ran as fast as we could and my ribs were still hurting. It was almost impossible for me to breathe. The guys were ahead of me now and Rukus was a few inches away. I spotted the 6 train station up ahead on Lexington and 58th Street. Our only way of not getting caught by the Satunian army was going underground. We headed towards the subways, and jumped over the fare gates. There weren't any MTA crew members around to stop us either. Rukus and his cyclops followed us inside. They slowed down a little bit, due to the unfamiliar underground station.

"Hurry! I have an idea!" I shouted.

It was actually a way out. We were going to have to take a big risk doing so.

There was an empty train at this stop and one of the doors was propped open halfway. We all got inside and headed to the next wagon, then the next until we got to the first car. We ran to the conductor's station and it was locked.

Uh oh.

"What now?" Bruce asked, frightened.

"Erick, they're gaining on us!" Luis warned.

"Hurry! Hand me something. I need to smash the door handle open!" I exclaimed. The guys were all searching for something useful I could use, but they didn't find anything. We were trapped.

"Quick! Keep 'em out!" Patrick yelled.

Bruce and Larry both ran to the other side of the car, and held on to the metal door handles. The demons were punching the doors with force. Good thing the glass was tough enough to withstand such impacts.

"Hurry, we can't keep them out much longer," Larry said still holding on.

"Everyone get out of the way," Patrick announced.

He came running fast with all his weight and smashed into the conductor's door. The first try left a dent on it, the second try, some of the hinges came off, then the last try, the whole door came down. I had no idea Patrick was this strong, and neither did I have the time to thank him either. I had to run inside to the control room and figure out a way to start the train. I hit a few buttons, and placed my hand on the lever from the right corner of the controllers.

I figured that was for speed.

"Everyone get off the train on my count," I instructed. "Luis? Get to that door and open it."

Luis ran to one of the side doors and tried to get it open. I pushed the lever upwards and the train started moving forward, slowly at first, but then started gaining speed, fast. Luis finally got the side door open, just in time for us to jump off. Mathcus jumped out first, then Bruce. I was next, then Larry and Jimmy both let go of the handle and jumped off the train as well.

The train sped up fast.

The demons were still trapped inside the train with no driver. Who knows where they were headed. Hopefully China or something.

We were all gasping for air.

"I'm impressed, chief," Larry said. I bobbed my head in acknowledgment.

"That was close though," I replied

"Yeah, let's not do that again," Patrick suggested rubbing his right arm.

"Let's get the heck out of here," Jimmy suggested.

We all got out of the station and the area was clear. The Satunians weren't marching around this area.

"We need to find the girls and my grandfather, so let's split up," I said.

"I'll go find them," Larry volunteered.

"I'll go with you," Luis said.

"What about you?" Larry asked.

"I need to find a friend," I responded. Matheus glanced at me after I said that.

"What if he has already evacuated?" Larry asked curiously.

"I have a feeling he hasn't," I assured him. "Meet us here when you find them and be careful, alright?"

"Tato," Luis said. Which means 'Okay,' in his Spanish slang.

Both Larry and Luis headed back to the Midtown Tunnel. Meanwhile, the rest of us ran down to 49th Street and 7th Avenue. I led the way towards a very nice fancy building. The door was wide open with no doorman at the entrance. We went inside the building, and noticed that the elevators weren't working either.

"What floor is it again?" Patrick was the first one to ask.

"10th," I replied.

"You're kidding right?" Bruce exclaimed.

I shot him a serious look.

"I guess you're not kidding!"

I turned to Jimmy and Patrick, asking for any volunteers, but they both ignored me and stared at the ceiling.

"I would've gone with you, but you already know I won't get too far," Patrick said, grabbing a chunk of skin from his stomach, which was a reasonable excuse.

"Why don't we rock paper scissors," Bruce suggested, standing in the middle of the hallway, with his hands ready.

"Forget it, I'll go by myself, alone, in the dark, with demons lurking around trying to kill me." I added, expecting sympathy. They weren't changing their minds though.

"I guess, it's me and you then," Matheus said.

"We can duck duck goose," Bruce also recommended.

"Just stay here," I said, which was exactly what they were going to do.

Matheus and I headed up the stairs. As soon as we got to the 5th floor, I was already dying.

"Tired already?" Matheus teased.

"Look, pooch, I'm not used to this, okay? As a matter of fact..." I had to stop talking to catch my breath. "You should change into big bird again, and fly me up there," I finished as we kept going up the stairs.

"Sorry, I'm not used to flying lazy people on my back."

Stupid dog.

Finally, we had reached the 10th floor and I couldn't feel my legs anymore. Once I recovered, we went into the hall and I searched for apartment 10F.

I knocked a few times, and someone answered the door.

THANK GOD.

"Erick?" Craig said, staggered to see me "What are you doing here, kid? Where's Jack?" he asked, concerned. He let us in the apartment.

"I came here looking for you. We got separated on the island," I informed him.

"You were what? The island? What the hell were y'all doing

there? The team and I were waiting for you guys in Africa for two days. We thought something went wrong, and I tried reaching you guys but I couldn't get through. What in the world happened?"

"Nathan betrayed us, and we got ourselves in a huge mess after that."

"Please tell me you guys have nothing to do with what's going on out there."

"Well, umm, sort of," was my answer.

"Holy smokes! HA! You guys screwed things up this time. Wow! So Jack actually found Satu?" he said, smiling.

"Yeah, but it's not looking good. There's an army of demons out there ready to kill and wipe out our entire city. We can't let that happen, Craig. We need to find my parents immediately. They're the only ones that might know how to stop this."

Craig paced back and forth, thinking. He looked like he had something in mind. "Come with me," he said. We walked down the hallway, back to the elevators. He called an elevator up and surprisingly, it was working.

WHAT THE...?

"I thought the elevators weren't working," I said.

"They are; they're just not stopping on the first floor for some reason."

I can't believe I went up 10 flights of stairs for nothing. I heard furball giggling behind me. I looked back and rolled my eyes at him. We got on the elevator and went up to the rooftop.

When we got to the 40th floor, Craig left the elevator and we followed. I had a perfect view of the city. Couldn't really say it was beautiful, since some of the buildings were destroyed. Even the Chrysler building was falling apart. In the distance, I could also see the Brooklyn Bridge collapsing.

"This is bad," Craig said, looking at the bridge too. We continued walking towards a blue and silver colored Bell helicopter. Craig got in it, and started messing with some controls. He turned on the helicopter's radio, and switched it to the emergency frequency channel.

"This is 3227 to 518, over?" He repeated the transmission twice.

No answer.

He said it one more time, and there was static.

"Ov—This is—" a voice replied.

"518? This is 3227, repeat that last transmission, over?"

"Copy, this is 51—over?"

"Matt? Is that you?" There was more static. "Matt? Do you hear me? Over."

"Yeah, Craig, loud and clear."

"What is your exact location?" Craig asked.

"38° 00' N and 97° 00' W, copy." Craig took out a map from one of the compartments, and examined it. He turned to me with a smile. He seemed happy.

"They're on their way back," he said to me, then turned back to the radio. "How many passengers in your craft?"

It took me a minute to realize that the Matt he was speaking to was the Hawker pilot that flew us to Detarru Island.

"4 passengers, copy?" Matt answered.

"Are the Ross family there with you? Over." There was silence. "Matt come in, over."

I turned to Matheus, but he didn't seem worried.

"Yes, sir, both Mr. and Mrs. Ross are in my craft, but not the boy," he answered, referring to me.

"That's a copy. What's your time of arrival?"

"1800 hours, over." Craig looked at his watch and it was 4 pm. "They'll be here soon. Get in." He turned on the engine and I got in the helicopter next to him with Matheus.

"Craig? We need to get my friends first!" I shouted. He couldn't hear me because of the engines. He motioned to put on the helicopter headphones.

We both did.

"We need to get my friends," I repeated, as I pointed downwards.

He got the point.

He lifted the helicopter up in the air, gained some speed, and then turned a few degrees, trying to keep the chopper away from the building. He flew around it, descending, trying to figure out which side of the street he could land on. He found the perfect spot.

When he landed, I got off the craft and ran to get my friends. I had to run around the block, since the entrance to the building was on the other side.

"Guys?" I called and they all came running out of the building. As we ran back, the female demon from before was blocking our way back to the helicopter. I was horrified to see her again.

It happened so fast, not even my friends saw it coming. All I could remember was her standing there, and then saw myself being dragged up in the air.

It was faster than light.

She lifted me up by the front of my shirt, then carried me by the stomach. I heard Jimmy shouting, and then saw Bruce running towards the helicopter to get Matheus.

The demon was so fast, it felt like I was on a roller coaster ride. We flew over the city for a few minutes.

"Hey! Let go!"

She ignored my demands.

"Let me go, I said!"

I didn't technically mean to let go, 60 stories high up in the air, yet she did let go, and now I was going to fall on my head from this altitude. Chances of surviving this fall were 0%.

"Oh God! Take me back, take me back!" I screamed desperately, as I was falling. I almost peed myself there too.

She took a second to consider my request, then she caught me by my foot. I was upside down, dangling in the air.

"Are you crazy?" I screamed at her. "Why would you let go of me?"

She looked down at me for a second, not responding.

Note to self: Never, ever ask her to do that again.

"Are you always like this?" She finally spoke.

"How? Upside down? 1,000 feet above ground? Absolutely!" I responded sarcastically. She looked down at me again and had a grin on her face. "At least you have a sense of humor."

"Considering what you did to me? Trust me, if I were you, I wouldn't let my guard down for one second."

I was kind of pushing it though. Hanging the way I was, and knowing what she's capable of, I think it was smarter to keep my mouth shut.

She was pretty good at not showing her emotions. Or perhaps she just knew how to ignore me. She started descending and she was heading to a nearby building.

"Where are you taking me?"

I felt blood rushing to my head from being upside down for so long. I waited until she got closer to ground to break free. When she did, I reached up to my foot and struggled to remove her grip. She let go and I fell, hurting my lower back again.

Dang it.

If I wasn't careful enough, I'd probably end up paralyzed after all this was over.

I looked over my shoulder and saw the demon was standing a few feet away, staring down at me with one hand on her hip. I slowly got on my feet, ready to make a run for it again.

"Relax! I'm not going to hurt you," she reassured. I didn't know whether to believe her or not. Besides, I didn't trust her one bit.

"Nice try, witch. You stay the heck away from me, you hear?" I threatened with my knuckles up, ready to fight. She didn't seem to be bothered at anything I said, which was odd.

"I have information you need."

"What makes you think I need it?" I replied, skeptical.

"Because it is about Satu."

She had my attention. "Why are you helping me?"

"Because I'm better off helping you than him."

"Do you expect me to believe that? You're just going to turn against your own? Just like that?"

"Listen, I just wanted to give you a heads up. Satu is not only after Earth. What Satu is really after—"

"He's after The Order, I know that already, tell me something I don't know," I interrupted rudely.

"Precisely why I came to you. He thinks I'm oblivious to his foolish agenda. He's going to use your friends as pawns so he can be crowned as a devil."

That struck me. I gulped so hard, I almost choked on my own saliva.

"It doesn't make any sense. He has an entire army, so why use my friends for that?" I asked.

"You do realize your friends are not ordinary humans, right?"

"Well, yeah, but—"

"These friends of yours are really archangels."

"Archangels?" I faltered.

"Just one of them could cause tremendous damage. Combine them all together, and you'll have a lethal weapon against humanity, and even the underworld. That's the reason why he's so desperate to find them."

Such intel had me trembling with horror.

"How is he planning on doing this?"

"At the moment, he's searching for them, but once he has all five archangels, he's planning to control them with a so-called Book of Mythos, she said, smacking me with more shocking information.

"The Book of Mythos?" I repeated.

Do my friends even know the powers they possess? Do they even know what they are?

"Who are you? Why are you helping me?"

"My name is Lola. I am The Master Chief of Inferno and I am in charge of all its Dimensions. There is a barrier between demons and devils, which cannot be crossed. Demons have been taking orders from devils for as long as hell was created. I'm definitely not pleased with the idea of taking orders from that insignificant fool."

She didn't like him very much by the sound of things. "So why are you helping him?"

"We made a deal. In the beginning, I thought his intentions were to rule Earth. If I provided him with an army, he would give me half of this territory. Unfortunately, that is not the case anymore."

"This territory is my home. Look what you've done, you've destroyed it. Many innocent people have lost their lives because of you," I said, furious.

"I'll take full responsibility for my actions. However, my demons haven't killed anyone yet."

I glanced at her, surprised to hear the good news.

"They still injured a lot of people, Lola."

"Like I said, I'll take full responsibility for my actions. Right now, you have to come with me."

I paced back and forth, thinking about my options. Should I trust her?

"Okay, on one condition and one condition only," I finally answered.

"What are your terms?"

"When this is over, you'll answer to my superiors." I didn't even know who my superiors were, but I wanted her to know I wasn't alone.

She agreed.

CHAPTER 15

"WHAT HAPPENED TO HIM?" Kate shouted, worried, as soon as she heard the news about Erick.

"It's our fault," Bruce said disappointed. "We shouldn't have left him alone."

"It's nobody's fault," Matheus said. "It happened too fast, and no one saw it coming."

"It's crucial that we find him. Isn't there a way for you to track him?" Harris asked Matheus.

"I can't. She flew off with him."

"What about our powers, Harris? They've been gone since our last battle on Detarru Island," Jimmy added.

"I know. The Creator took them away, for reasons I do not understand. Yet, I do not question him and I do not doubt for one second that he is helping us carry out this task as we speak. I know you will get your powers back when the time is right."

Everyone stood there silent, trying to come up with any ideas.

Kate was really concerned about Erick. She only had met him that morning, and she was already fond of him. She loved his personality and his willpower. She loved the way he handled himself, his kindness and caring for others, and his good spirit. She also felt sorry for him though, since he had such an enormous responsibility.

"Which way did she go?" Kate asked, breaking the silence.

"That way," Bruce said, pointing north.

Kate was deep in thought.

"Why would she kidnap him now? It doesn't make any sense." She was talking to herself. She looked up at the guys.

"We need to go north," she suggested.

"But he could be anywhere," Larry said.

"It's impossible to find him without our powers," Luis also said.

"We need to try," Kate said with a firm voice. "You guys were chosen to protect The Order, right? Standing around like idiots, waiting for something to happen, is not helping Erick or any of us. Your powers were taken away, yes, but that doesn't make you handicapped. Erick is the youngest of this group, and look how far he's gotten on this mission without any powers. Why can't you? He's been following his instincts, and so far he has done an amazing job at it. Archangels or not, maybe it's time for you to start applying those skills and be human for once."

Those were strong words, but Kate did have a point, and they all acknowledged her for that.

It was a lesson learned.

"She's right," Jimmy exclaimed and turned to the guys. "You heard the lady. Let's get moving, this fight is not over yet."

Larry walked up to her and kissed her on the cheek. "Thank you," he said smiling, which threw her off a bit. She wasn't expecting that from her grumpy older brother. Knowing she was helping them filled her up with joy.

"Craig is on his way to Erick's parents," Harris spoke. "We'll know about Plan B once they get here. For now, we need to focus on our mission. We all have a job to do and right now, Erick is our number one priority."

Everyone agreed.

6:10pm

The Hawker arrived at the private airport. Clara and Jack both got out of the plane and met with Craig, who was outside waiting for them by his Bell helicopter.

"Craig? Have you heard from him?" Clara called. Craig glanced at them as they waited desperately for an answer.

"He was with me, about an hour ago and—"

"Where is he? Is he alright?" Jack asked, concerned.

"I don't know, I—"

"What happened, Craig? Where is he?" Clara asked.

"We were going to come get you, but we got separated when he went back to get his friends."

"His friends?" she asked.

"Yes, a couple of kids, around his age."

Clara looked at Jack and smiled. "He finally found The Others! Was my father with him?"

"Your father? I thought he passed away. Please explain to me what the hell is going on here?"

"It's a long story. My father and The Others should be searching for Erick now. Can you take us there?"

"Sure, come on."

As they both turned to get in the helicopter, they saw Matt get out.

"Matt, are you coming?" Craig asked.

"I'm heading back," he said.

"Where?"

"The island. I need to find Milo." He went back inside and Rebecca and Nathan came out of the plane. Craig glanced at them, puzzled.

"You brought them here?"

"I guess you heard," Jack said.

"Yes, Erick told me everything, including how he put a gun to his head and forced him into the underworld."

"We couldn't just leave them back on the island, Craig," Clara said.

"Well, they are not coming with us now."

Nathan overheard Craig's comments. He walked up to them with Rebecca. "Sorry to interrupt, but we need to talk."

"We already talked about this, Nathan," Jack replied.

"You need to hear me out, Jack. Please, let me join you."

"Absolutely not," Craig interrupted.

"Look, I did this. I know I screwed things up, but give me a chance to fix it, please."

"Okay, Nathan, I'm gonna give you the benefit of the doubt, just be very careful because if anything happens to Erick or anyone else gets hurt, I will personally take care of you myself," Craig warned, then got in the helicopter. Clara followed.

Jack stared at both Rebecca and Nathan in disappointment, then got in the helicopter too.

THE METROPOLITAN MUSEUM OF ART

"There it is!" Lola said, pointing at a structure made out of bronze, similar to the one on the island. "This is the portal he's using to let my demons into your world."

"There is a similar one on Detarru Island, which is how I got into Inferno."

"I know. I was the one who gave the orders to bring you in when you were in Purgatory," she informed me. "Satu will be using these gates to have my demons spread globally."

"There has to be a way to stop this," I said.

"Precisely why I brought you here. I have a plan, but you might not like it."

"Okay? Shoot."

"Satu knows that if he captures you, your friends will come here looking for you."

"We can't let him," I said, worried. "We need to warn them."

"I can't do that."

"Why not?"

"He asked me to bring you in myself. So, if I don't, he will be suspicious of me and realize I'm helping you. I know he's got an eye on me ever since I questioned him about The Others. He knows I'm on to him, and I can't raise any more suspicion."

"So how are we supposed to stop him from getting to my friends and using them to destroy The Order?"

"Like I said, you won't like my idea, but you're going to have to trust me, Ethasus, or it will be over before you even know it."

I looked at her for a minute. She meant business. It was either that or losing this battle. I sure didn't like the idea, but I didn't want to see thousands of innocent people lose their lives because of me either. I had to rely on my instincts once more and make a decision. Of course, one of those decisions was going to turn out to be an inevitable oblivion.

Which one? I'd have to find out myself.

"Alright, tell me what you need me to do."

Downtown Manhattan

"Look, guys! Look at that building over there!" Kate pointed at a massive building a few blocks away.

"Wait, isn't that The Metropolitan Museum of Art?" Jimmy asked.

"It is!" Luis confirmed.

"It hasn't been touched yet, why?" Kate asked.

"I kinda have the feeling Erick is in there," Patrick said.

"Me too," Larry also said.

"He is!" Matheus confirmed. He started sniffing the air. He could smell Erick from a mile away.

"Good work, guys! Now let's hurry and get him out of there," Harris said.

The Metropolitan Museum of Art

My hands were tied up behind my back. Lola dragged me by the arm while we were walking down the long corridors of the museum. The artifacts, the arts, the sculptures and the paintings, were untouched.

We made it through a few more rooms.

I forgot how huge this place was. You'd end up lost in here if you didn't have a tour map. Security was tight in here too.

There were like 10 Satunians guarding the museum in every room. Lola kept dragging me a bit too harshly. That was her idea of making it look real.

We had finally arrived in a large room with a gigantic dome on the ceiling. Sitting in front of us was this bald and pale guy. His eyes were shut. I thought he was taking a nap or something. He was also wearing a cape.

Talk about ridiculous. Who would wear something like that?

"Here! Just as you requested, Satu," Lola said.

That one moment when you start to twitch for no reason.

He opened his eyes; they were silver gray, and he had an evil glare.

It felt like he was staring right through me. I was trembling and in shock. My heart was beating so fast, I thought it was going to explode.

Right in front of me was the enemy, and he was just a few feet away from killing me. The person I was supposed to fight for the second time in history, yet he didn't look familiar to me at all. He looked tough though, and I'm not going to lie, I was SO FREAKING SCARED.

He got up from his chair and walked towards me. He was muscular alright, with big hands. The type of hands you could just crush someone's head with.

Every step he took made my heart beat faster. I really regretted listening to Lola. I should've taken option 2. I should've just said no.

"Ethasus! It is nice to see you again, alive and well," he lied. Even his voice was scary. I really wanted to go home. I really started wishing I had no part in this fight whatsoever. Why couldn't I just be a normal guy? Why did I have to fight this guy? Why me?

He took a few more steps, trying to take a closer look at me.

"Still look like that weak little boy I met once on the island. You haven't changed a bit. I just don't understand how someone like you could have possibly succeeded? I had you. I could've just stabbed you in the heart with my sword. Just could've done so many things to you. Yet, you still defeated me. You know what your biggest mistake was? The day you had me imprisoned in Purgatory thinking I would never get out, and hunt you down."

When he said those last words, he clenched his teeth, like dogs do ready to bite your face off. He reached out, grabbed my shirt, and with his grip, pulled me closer to his face.

"I have been waiting far too long for this moment, Ethasus. The moment when you will witness your world crumble down in pieces. When you'll witness your guardians dying before your eyes, and where I'll watch the light leave your eyes once I kill you," he snarled with a grin.

"Found him a few blocks away. The Others should be here any minute now," Lola interrupted.

He looked at her perplexed for a moment. I think he was so fixed on me he had forgotten about her presence.

"Good job! Is your army in place?" he asked, turning his attention back to me.

"Affirmative. Waiting for your command."

She never mentioned she had a whole army of cyclops ready to ambush my friends.

"What are you doing?" I asked her. "This was not—"

She slapped me across the face really hard. That shut me up good.

"What would you like me to do with him?" she asked quickly.

Satu found her behavior really strange. He kept staring at both of us, and studying us.

"Leave him here, with me." He walked back to his chair.

"Negative."

Satu turned and glared at her with such intensity.

"You do remember our deal? Right?" she asked.

"If I remember clearly, you wanted him alive in exchange for The Others," he replied.

"Exactly! I do not trust you alone with him. Not after what I just witnessed. So forgive me, but I think I should have the privilege to keep an eye on my price."

She sure saved me from this lunatic.

"You are always ahead of your game, Lola. Very well then, do as you please, but he's not allowed to leave this building."

"Of course," she agreed, then grabbed me by the arm again, and dragged me away.

The Detarrunians

"This should be the place," Craig announced, while hovering over the streets of Downtown Manhattan in his helicopter.

"I don't see them," Jack said.

"They must be looking for Erick," Clara stated while they kept flying over the city. Craig noticed a massive crowd in black clothing standing around, waiting for something.

"Who are these people?"

"They must be the Satunians," Rebecca broke in.

"Why are the Satunians in New York?"

"Looks like they know about Plan B." Clara added, "Hurry, take us to Madison Square Garden!"

"What about Erick?" Craig asked.

"I trust my father will find him, but right now you need to take me to my mother."

"Your mother? Isn't she in California?"

"I lied about that too, Craig. She's been in New York for a few years, preparing our Detarrunian Army."

"Well I'll be damned! You guys are full of surprises. So what is plan A?"

Jack and Clara looked at each other, not knowing who would answer the question first.

"Plan A is Erick," she answered.

"What about him?"

"He is The Chosen One."

"Get the hell out!? How come you guys didn't mention this before?" He was awestruck.

"I didn't even know either, until two days ago," Jack said. "I just also found out that Clara was a guardian."

"You guys got some serious explaining to do," Craig said as he turned the helicopter around.

The Search

"Remember! We get Erick, and then we get the heck out of there. We don't have our powers, so don't try to be heroes," Jimmy said as they all hid behind a big chunk of wall on the street. "If we get separated, we'll meet back at the Midtown Tunnel, understand?"

Everyone nodded and they strolled up a few stairs towards the museum's front entrance.

"Matheus? Let us know if it's clear to go inside," Harris instructed.

Matheus sneaked inside the door, and surprisingly, it was open. There weren't any Satunians or demons guarding it either. He came right back and signaled it was clear. They all cautiously sneaked inside.

"Alright, this place is divided into two buildings. We're going to have to split up," Patrick suggested whispering.

"Harris? You should stay out here with the girls," Larry advised.

"Then I'll search building 1 with you, Larry," Jimmy volunteered. "Matheus, you're with us. Patrick, Luis, and Bruce, you'll search Building 2."

"Are you sure you guys will be okay?" Kate asked, troubled.

"We'll be fine," Larry responded confidently.

They went separate ways, searching for Erick.

CHAPTER 16

THE METROPOLITAN MUSEUM OF ART

"WHY DIDN'T YOU TELL me you were going to ambush my friends?" I shouted, upset.

Lola was in the room with me, supposedly holding me prisoner. This was the part of the museum where they kept mummified corpses and Egyptian replicas.

I really hated mummies.

"I did tell you," she responded in dismay.

"But you failed to tell me that you were planning to hurt them?"

"I already told you, my cyclops won't harm anyone unless I tell them to."

"What is Satu going to do to them?" I was not shutting up, and I think I was aggravating her for the first time.

She actually rolled her eyes at me. She walked past me towards a window in the room.

"Where are you going?"

"I'm going to check up on your friends, and make sure Satu doesn't hurt them, maybe then you'll shut up for once"

GEEZ.

"Hey! Are you just going to leave me in here?" I was horrified at the thought of that. I sure didn't want to be left alone in this place with psychopath Satu around.

"Absolutely," she responded flatly.

"But what if he comes and tries to kill me again?"

"Don't worry, I'll leave my pets to watch over you, just in case." She flew off to I don't know where, and left me there alone.

"Her pets?" I said to myself.

My worst nightmare crawled in from the same window Lola had flew off from. The same flesh-eating, blood-sucking creatures that tormented me for years in Inferno, and there were four of these things coming in the room.

Freaking hollows.

I ran to the door and it was locked from the outside.

Of course it was, I was a prisoner.

It was like being back in Inferno all over again, back to being tortured. I'm going to die, I thought. Why would Lola do this to me?

Those things surrounded me while my back was up against the door. I was gasping for air and those things gazed at me while smelling living flesh right in front of them. Their long tongues dropped, trying to taste the air or taste fear, which I was releasing in barrels. I tried to stay calm and not provoke them. I thought that if I stayed calm, they would think of me as a Satunian or something.

They looked hungry too. Hungry killing creatures, ready to jump on me any time, regardless of how calm I was.

I heard the doorknob turning. Someone unlocked the door and slightly opened it. It was enough to peek inside and I saw someone.

Larry?

I jumped out the door, and got out so fast, I don't think it was even physically possible. I grabbed Larry by the arm, and I ran so fast that while I was running, I saw Jimmy and Matheus waving at me but I didn't know how to stop myself to warn them.

"Erick? Where are you going?" Larry shouted as he ran next to me.

"I don't know, just run," I warned, while looking back at the guys who were still standing there puzzled.

"AAHH!" I heard them all scream after they saw those hideous things too. They also ran behind us.

We ran for about a minute then looked back again, and didn't see them behind us anymore.

THANK GOD.

"I think we lost them," I said, stopping to catch my breath.

"Are you sure?" Larry asked, horrified. We stood there quietly, trying to listen carefully for danger, but there was none.

"To think that we came here to save you," Jimmy said, still breathing fast.

"I think you just saved us," Larry concluded chuckling.

We started walking again and found it really strange that there were no Satunians around. Where did everyone go?

Luis, Bruce and Patrick bumped into us.

"Erick!" Patrick said happy to see me.

I didn't see Pops and the girls though. "Where's the rest of the group?" I asked.

"They're waiting outside," Jimmy said.

We ran out of the building, but there was no sign of them.

"They said they'd wait out here," Bruce explained. "They probably went inside looking for you."

I didn't like that answer.

"Listen, just get out of here, guys. Satu is planning to use you to destroy The Order."

No one believed me. Matheus wasn't even aware of such intel either.

"How do you know that?" he asked.

"Lola told me."

"Who's Lola?"

"Lola is the demon that kidnapped me," I said.

"And why would you believe her?"

"Satu knows about their powers, Matheus. He knows they're archangels, and he's planning to use that power against me and the whole world."

"Good heavens! Why would he want to do something like that? For what reasons?" Matheus said baffled.

"He wants to become a devil."

"You trust that demon?" Matheus asked, concerned.

"So far Lola's been very helpful to me. She has a plan that can be beneficial to all of us and I trust her on this. Something tells me I should. This is our only chance. She has control over her demons and if I could gain her trust, she can keep her demons from hurting innocent people. Besides, she doesn't really want Satu to succeed."

"What makes you so sure?" Luis asked.

"Because if he becomes a devil, that would only mean she's bound to him for all eternity. Trust me, she doesn't like the idea."

"Well that part is believable," Matheus confirmed.

"If he captures you all, it's game over," I said.

"We came here to get you out, Erick. We can't go back without you now!" Larry exclaimed.

"Don't worry, I'll have Matheus with me."

At first they were about to argue, especially Jimmy and Larry, but they knew there were greater risks if they got captured.

I didn't realize how much these guys cared so much for me. So much they would risk it all just to save me, which was making things a little more complicated. Besides trying to save the world, I also had to keep in mind that these guys were counting on me.

As I stood there in silence, lost in my own thoughts, I saw that Matheus got a bit edgy all of a sudden.

"Something is wrong, Ethasus," Matheus said in a very low voice.

"What is it?"

"Something is not right. I can feel them. Their powers are back," he said with his ears straight in alert.

"I don't understand." I turned to them to see what Matheus was talking about.

The guys were just standing there, idle. It was like they were possessed or something.

"Someone has awakened their powers."

"I thought they had their powers to begin with?" I said confused.

"No. Their powers were taken away by The Creator, but this is definitely bad timing."

I was about to walk up to them. "Don't! Stay away from them," he warned.

"What's wrong with them?"

"They're under Satu's control now," came a voice from behind us. It was Lola. She had Kate, Sarah and my grandfather tied up and gagged.

"What is this?" I yelled.

She didn't respond.

"I thought we had a deal!" I was angry now.

A bunch of Satunians and cyclops appeared out of nowhere and surrounded us. I guess this was the ambush she warned me about. I should've seen it coming.

Dang it.

"Excellent work, Lola!" came a familiar voice from behind the crowd of Satunians and demons. They all parted, making way for Satu. He walked to the front of the circle, with The Book of Mythos in his hands. He laughed at us, especially at me.

I felt so used and betrayed. I can't explain this embarrassing feeling. It was the kind where you have no choice but to admit that you're a failure, and there is not a thing you can do about it. These guys were counting on me and I let them down. It was all my fault. I was definitely not worthy of my calling. I just couldn't do one thing right.

Satu was going to use my archangels and he had them under his control now.

What was I supposed to do? I really wished my grandfather was able to help me. I needed his guidance, but he was a bit tied up at the moment.

"How does it feel to lose?" Satu asked, walking towards me with his hands crossed behind his back, and a smirk on his face. I really wanted to cut his face off. "Your arrogance deceived you this time, Ethasus. You underestimated my intelligence once more and now, you have failed."

I didn't say a word. I was really down and upset at myself. It's like my soul didn't have energy to keep going. If I were home, I would suffer from depression and sleep my life away under my pillow.

"What's the matter? Can't bear your future?" he snickered.

"Why try to conquer the world and later destroy it? What is your purpose?" I asked. "Why kill so many for immortality when you already have it? What is it that you want?"

I really needed to know. I needed to know if there was something provoking him and causing him to do such atrocities. Maybe I could convince him not to do this. Perhaps change his mind.

I was willing to try. I would do anything to save humanity. There is no way this guy just woke up one day and decided to kill everyone and everything.

"You think this is about immortality? This is about power. This is about overthrowing whoever is in charge. Destroying The Order is the first step to success. Without you getting in my way, Hell and Heaven will collapse, and sooner or later, there will be no higher power. I will be the only God in town. I'll create my own worlds, my own hells, and my own kingdoms. It will eventually be all about me." He had a foul grin.

This guy was seriously insane. It wasn't about being a devil anymore. He wanted to be

THE DEVIL.

"Do you realize that if the order is destroyed, you can rest assured that more of these archangels will come looking for you, and they're going to kill you," I warned, trying to put some sense into him.

"They'll make sure that never happens." He pointed at my friends.

"You're pathetic. No Book of Mythos is going to stop the wrath of the gods. You are making a huge mistake, and dude, you are going to be so screwed." I shook my head in dismay.

He despised me more than ever.

His glares were piercing through my skull. I had to look away a few times. He was sure an intimidating guy. He got closer to me and I looked at Matheus, thinking he was going to kill me now.

"You know, I really wanted to be nice, and put you out of your misery, but now, it is way more satisfying to kill you last. This way, you'll be forced to watch how I terminate this world you so passionately love. You have underestimated me for the last time, Ethasus. Now I'm going to show you what I am capable of because I'm not someone you want to screw with. Here is a little demonstration of what you'll be witnessing in just a few hours. I think this should be fun to watch."

He turned to the guys who were still standing there stalling. It's like they weren't even there or even conscious. He gave a command with his hand, and Larry woke up from idleness. He walked right past me and didn't even acknowledge me. He walked towards my grandfather who was tied up next to Kate and Sarah.

"Larry?" I called "Larry, what are you doing?"

It was unexpected, I didn't even see it coming. I couldn't stop him, even if I wanted to. Larry punched my grandfather so hard in the chest that he flew up in the air and hit the wall. Seconds later he dropped to the floor.

"Pops?" I screamed. I ran to him and picked him up in my arms. He didn't respond. I searched for a pulse but there was none. The force on his chest stopped his heart right away.

My grandfather was dead.

I was so shockingly disturbed, I couldn't breathe. Even Matheus stood still.

Everything felt so different. I couldn't move and my body couldn't register. The only thing I could do was cry. I couldn't help it. It was a horrible feeling. A feeling of sorrow and guilt. I was supposed to be strong, but this wasn't fair. The pain in my chest was unbearable. Why him?

As I was sobbing, Larry headed for Kate next. He picked her up by her shirt. He was going to kill her too.

"Wait, Larry!" I ran to him, trying to stop him. "Don't do this."

He turned, and hit me square on the jaw. He almost knocked me out. I hit the floor disoriented.

He turned back to Kate, grabbed her by the throat and started choking her to death with one hand.

"Larry stop, please, don't do this!"

I felt two hands grab me from behind. It was Satu.

"How does it feel?" he whispered in my ear. "You did this, Ethasus. You killed them."

"No!" I screamed.

"Yes!" he teased, laughing

"Let go of me!"

I didn't even have the energy to fight it anymore.

"Larry," I pleaded while tears came out. I was crying again. There was nothing I could do to stop this madness. I watched hopelessly as my whole life changed drastically right before my eyes.

Kate was almost passing out. Matheus finally reacted and went after Larry while turning into a Phoenix again. He flew by Larry and with his wing, flung him up in the air. He landed on top of a few cyclops. Matheus instantly flew back to Kate and Sarah and carried my grandfather with his beak. He then grabbed both Kate and Sarah with his feet.

"Hurry Matheus! Get out of here!" I yelled. He flew off with them, getting them away from danger. A few cyclops went after them.

"They won't escape me. They are going to die no matter what you do," he mocked while letting go of my arms.

I turned and swung at him but he dodged all of my punches.

I wasn't even swinging that hard to be honest. All I wanted was to keep him away from me.

"Get it through that little head of yours. You will not win this battle, boy."

I wasn't even listening anymore. He had done enough. My head was somewhere else and my emotions were out of control.

One moment, I was scared and sad, and another I was completely filled with rage. I was going to find a way to make him pay for this. This was far from over.

"Take him away," Satu ordered.

Two Satunians walked towards me. They were going to grab my arms but I found an opening and ran inside the museum.

"Get him!" I heard Satu yell.

I made a few turns, remembering the room Lola had showed me before, and I ran inside The Gates of Hell.

I was back in Inferno.

The Army

"I can't believe all of these people are Erick's Army," Craig exclaimed, looking at such multitude.

They were all in Madison Square Garden. They'd been preparing for this very day. Some of these people were born and raised on the island, the rest were regular New Yorkers and people from other parts of the world who decided to join after this whole thing went down. Injured men, women, and children were being attended on one side of the massive building, while most of them were heavily armed. They had an entire arsenal, which was being provided by hundreds of military personnel. Martial Law took over the city, and outside of the coliseum were about 20 war tanks. This army could wipe out the Satunians in minutes, but then again, they didn't know what they were up against. They had to be extra cautious, since Satu would do anything to win.

There were people of authority at the center of the arena: Homeland Security, colonels, generals and other decision-making individuals from the State of New York. A few of them were talking directly to the President of The United States from a satellite phone.

Big monitors all over the coliseum were broadcasting the

news. People from all over the world were talking about the destruction of New York. Some displayed demons attacking innocent people on live TV, and the destruction of the Chrysler building and bridges.

"Come on, we need to find my mother," Clara said, trying to walk through the immense crowd. They followed her down to the center of the arena.

Once Clara and the rest finally made it to the center of the arena, they saw a lady wearing a red top and blue jeans. She seemed focused and determined but also stressed.

"Mom? Clara called. The lady turned, and soon as she saw her daughter, she smiled with joy and instantly hugged both Jack and Clara. She was very happy to see them, but her smile quickly disappeared when she realized that Erick wasn't with them.

"Where's Erick?"

"We were separated," Clara answered, saddened.

"He was your responsibility." Her voice changed.

"It wasn't her fault," Jack explained. "I'm the only one to blame. I hired unreliable people into my research and now all of this happened because I wasn't careful enough." He gave Nathan and Rebecca a mean glare.

"Yes, I know. You should've stopped searching for Satu a long time ago when we told you to," she strictly scolded.

"Look, Christine. No one mentioned to me that my own son was The Chosen One. If I would've known this, I wouldn't have put my son's life at risk. His identity shouldn't have been hidden from me, and as his father, I demand an explanation."

Christine stood quiet and didn't respond. He was right though. If he had only known about Erick, none of this would've happened.

"I'm sorry, Jack. Harris and I made the decision after he was born, but as you can see, it was a terrible mistake."

"Erick managed to find Dad in Paradise," Clara informed her, trying to ease the situation.

"Harris?!" she said, surprised. "Have you heard from him?"

"Yes! Erick's been with him and The Others this whole time," Craig added.

"So he finally found The Others!" She smiled again.

Christine walked up to one of the news reporters that was at the arena, interviewing eyewitnesses. She asked them to broadcast a message live. When her face was brought up on the big screens, everyone in the coliseum went silent. She took a few minutes to start her speech. There was anticipation from both parties. Even Clara and Jack wanted to know what Christine was about to say. They knew this speech was going to be seen all around the world. All nations were going to have to fight together for the sake of planet Earth.

"Difficult times await," she started. "I can only say that we must stay strong. We must come together as one. We mustn't let the Satunians take away our freedom. Many of you might think this is all a dream. Unfortunately, it's not. This is all real, and it's happening to us right now. We are at war, against people who believe that coexisting with demons is the right way to live. You can see for yourself what they've done to our city in just hours. Imagine what these creatures will do to our planet within days. Our people will be enslaved, and many souls will be sacrificed. We cannot allow this, for our children's sake. We Detarrunians have been trying to stop them for centuries, but each time, their numbers have grown. They've killed many of our people on Detarru Island and now, they are ready to do more damage in your cities. It's not about the island anymore; it's about taking over the entire world. If we don't stop them now, this will turn into an apocalyptical event, which will change our lives forever. If the Satunians win, there is going to be a war between gods and devils." She stopped for a second. Everyone was paying attention to her now.

"Christine? What happens when gods and devils fight each other?" one of the reporters asked in the back.

"It will be an endless ending," she replied. There was commotion. Some were talking about starting the war now, others were asking how to get rid of those demons. "This is why we have prepared ourselves," she continued. "This is why we are here. We have prepared an army to fight side by side with our guardians and The Chosen One. You can too. So, join our forces, and be a part of The Detarrunian Army. Our forces will combine, and we will be unstoppable. We will succeed, and we will send Satu and his demons back to hell!"

As soon as she said those words, the crowd started cheering and applauding. An immense roar was heard echoing around Grand Central, 32nd and 34th Street. Not only the people at Madison Square Garden were cheering but all around the world too.

This global army was ready for battle.

CHAP+ER 17

Inferno

I swear to my life; I was going to make him pay for this. My grandfather was going to be avenged, one way or another. I just couldn't go back right now. I refused to go back. I was ashamed of myself. I didn't even have the courage to face my friends or my family. I needed some time, and had to think things through. I had to get away from everyone and everything. This whole mission was too much for me. My grandfather was gone because of me, because of my wrong choices. I couldn't help but to think I was hopeless and how I let everyone down. I wanted to give up, but every time I did, I heard my grandfather's voice say:

'No matter what happens, never give up.'

How come the more I tried to do things right, the more I messed up?

I didn't want to go back. What for? To make things worse? I'd rather hide like a coward than face Satu.

Yes, I said it, I am a coward.

I heard a few demons flying in the distance. They were headed my way.

Christ! Why can't they just leave me alone?

I kept quiet and hid behind a big rock. I heard a familiar female voice talking to her demons as they all landed nearby.

"Ethasus? We know you're out there, come out. I need to speak with you."

How could I forget her? She was responsible for my grandfather's death.

That traitor.

I came out alright. I came at her so fast I was going to knock her out, but instead I tackled one of her goons who got in my way.

Whatever, as long as one of them got a beat down. As soon as he hit the ground with me on top of him, I punched him so hard in the eye. I think I killed him on the first punch, but I didn't care. I was going to kill the spirit out of him too.

If he had one.

Then I was going to kill it again and again. I kept punching it like a punching bag. The thing wasn't even moving anymore.

I felt two strong hands grab my arms and pull me away from him.

I screamed with rage. "Let me go!"

"Relax," she said calmly, letting go of my arms. I turned and swung at her. As usual, she was fast. She wanted me to stop but I wasn't listening and she wasn't fighting back either.

Good. Because I sure as hell was.

She flew up in the air trying to avoid my swings.

"Get down here and fight me, you coward. Let's end this right now!" I screamed. I saw the other demon standing there. I ran towards him, grabbed him by the wing and ripped it off. He moaned in pain. Then I kicked him hard in the stomach. He ran off scared and I was just about to run after him, but I was too tired. I fell to my knees, breathing hard.

"I'm not here to fight with you, Ethasus. I'm here to help you," she said.

"Haven't you done enough? You and Satu have ruined my life and he's about to destroy the world. Isn't that what you wanted?"

"That was Satu's own doing. I had nothing to do with that. I told you I wanted something entirely different. I did warn you about my plan, and you agreed to the terms, so why are you upset?"

"What do you want from me?" I asked, not caring anymore.

"My plan is not over yet."

"You want me to keep trusting you? After all that?"

"We need to trust each other, or we won't be able to win this."

"Say that to my dead grandfather."

"I told you, there was nothing I could do. Satu would've used The Others against me and killed me too."

"I can't help you anymore. My friends are under his control now. I can't fight against that kind of power."

"I know another way," she responded. I stood quiet, listening. She had my attention. "Aren't you going to ask me how?" she said with a sly smile.

"This isn't a game, Lola," I said in a low voice. I was angry again.

"Many will die. Get it through your head."

"If you would just listen to—"

"No," I interrupted. "I'm done listening to you. I trusted you once and everything you told me was a lie. I'll never trust you again so just leave me alone, I'm finished here." As I turned my back on her, she came at me with such strength, I didn't see it coming. She lifted me up in the air again and forced me to go with her.

HELL

Lola took me to the deepest and sinful of places. This place was in no way similar to Inferno. Inferno was darker, colder and swarming with all types of demons.

This place was submerged in evil and lava.

Literally.

My skin was on fire. I was burning alive. It wasn't burning my skin though. It was burning my soul.

It was awful.

The deeper we went, the more excruciating the pain was, but I had to endure it if I wanted retribution. I was willing to do anything, as long as Satu paid for what he did.

There were ruins and black temples, sort of like the ones in Greece but these were gigantic. They were dark and covered in lava.

Lola didn't seem to feel any pain though. I guess she was used to coming down here. We stopped by what seemed to be the end of the road of Hell. There was a massive hole at the center of this ocean. All the lava was pouring down like a water fall.

Where to? I couldn't tell. The hole was a seemingly dark abyss. Satan's dark abyss.

"Why are we here?" I asked, not trusting this demon one bit.

"I am going to introduce you to the only devil I trust."

"What? You really brought me here to meet Satan? What is wrong with you?" I screamed again. I wanted to run the heck out of there.

"Orcoptu is not Satan. Satan is a lot more powerful than Orcoptu and I don't even have the clearance to get to him."

"So why bring me here?"

"You need to convince him to join you," she replied.

"You want me to what? What makes you think he'll listen to me?"

I didn't know what was going on with this chick, but I finally realized she was psycho too.

"Let me be very clear," she warned. "Do not look into his eyes, do not speak before spoken to, and whatever you do, do not, I repeat, do not question him."

"What happens if I do?" I asked, trying to know the outcome.

"He'll eat your soul."

GULP.

Lola carried me up in the air, wrapped her wings around me, and we both made our way down into that black hole. Every minute, the heat and burns were more painful. We went on really deep into this warm hole.

After a few more minutes of torture, we finally made it to the bottom of this tormenting pit. The pain wasn't gone though. Now it was multiplied 100 times worst. The gravity in this place was unbearable and it was crushing my bones. The pressure in my head was killing me too and my lungs were going to collapse or explode.

There was a huge altar made out of black crystal and there were stones at the center of the place. Once we got near the altar, the pain went away. It was like magic.

Lola put me down and I was able to stand on my own two feet. As soon as I touched the ground, there was complete silence and nothing was heard. I couldn't even hear myself walking. It was weird.

I looked around the strange place. There was a throne made out of black crystals in the middle of the temple.

The temple was empty. Lola kept walking inside and I followed. When she got to the throne, Lola got on her knees and waited for someone. I did the same. We heard whispers echoing around the temple.

"Who disturbs me?" the voice said, whispering. I think I even felt a breeze behind my neck.

"It is I, Lola," she answered with reverence.

"I never called for you. What is your business here?"

"A human."

There was silence again, and I swear everything went dark for a minute.

A glowing gray smoke appeared before us, with an ugly death face.

Holy Jesus.

I couldn't see his eyes, but I saw his skeletal mouth with sharp gray teeth. His eyes were covered in gray mist. From where he was standing, he looked like one of those monsters from the movie Aliens. His right foot was shackled up with some underworld metal. He disappeared and then reappeared like an energy irregularity.

He reappeared behind me, and grabbed me from behind in a chokehold.

"How did he cross to the underworld?" the ugly devil asked while smelling my hair, curious to see a human for the first time. The guy was transparent, but he was strong. He grabbed my chin with his other hand and pulled my head back towards his shoulder. He seemed ready to bite my neck off.

I didn't want to die, so I yelled, "Lolaaaa!"

"He is not an ordinary human, my Lord. He is The Chosen One."

He stood there still holding on to my face. He had sharp white nails that could've slit my throat any minute. Telling this guy who I was definitely was not the smartest thing to do either. He growled like a beast and was ready to snap my head off.

"Satu wants to become a devil," she continued quickly. She wanted him to listen before he could break me in half.

She got his attention.

"That does not concern me," Orcoptu hissed.

"He wants to overthrow every devil in Hell. Ethasus is here to stop him, but he can't do it alone."

He let go of me and I fell to the ground. I backed away quickly from the thing and I ran behind Lola for safety.

"Do you have proof of such allegations?"

"He has five archangels under his control."

His face changed. I could finally see his eyes as they went wide with perplexity. They were white.

"He's planning to use them to destroy Earth and Paradise," she went on. "If Earth is destroyed—"

"The Order will be broken," he finished. He turned his back to us and walked up to his throne. He slowly sat and faced us again. I think he was looking at me. I felt his glare.

"So, The Order will be broken, and the war between devils and gods will begin. This is almost comical." He almost looked like he wanted this to happen. That didn't sound good. It wasn't looking too good for me either. This devil would probably join forces with Satu.

I couldn't let that happen.

I had to step my game up. I had to gain his alliance, otherwise it was game over. I had to say something. The gods confined him in Hell, but if freedom is what he wanted, then so be it.

"I... have a proposition," I stuttered, standing next to Lola. He quickly glared at me, furious. I even noticed how Lola glanced at me too. But I kept talking, even though she warned me not to speak.

"If you join forces with me—"

Orcoptu got out of his chair and stalked me. I was going to faint from fright. "Then what?" he asked while looking at me sideways. Well, I think he was looking at me sideways. I was trembling.

"I'll remove your shackles," I said backing up.

I could see him giving it some thought. "You don't have that kind of authority," he finally responded. He disappeared again and reappeared in front of me and grabbed me by the shirt so quickly, I didn't have time to react. The gray mist disappeared, revealing his white eyes again.

"The Creator will have to agree to my terms. I am the one risking my life to save all 6 realms!" I shouted.

"That's not good enough for me," he insisted. I saw him lifting an arm, ready to go for the kill.

I had to think of something and fast. Even if it cost me the most valuable thing I had.

"Then I'll sell you my soul," I bargained.

CHAPTER 18

EARTH

"I CAN'T BELIEVE YOU sold your soul to Orcoptu." Lola spoke first, after we made it back from Hell.

I didn't answer. Seems she was very staggered at my decision.

"Why?" Lola asked.

"Why what?"

"Why your soul?"

"I don't know, maybe out of desperation," I responded in a low voice. "Maybe I care too much for my friends and my family, I just can't let anything happen to them."

"I've never met anyone who would do what you just did, for the love of mankind. I just don't understand that."

"Well, you've never experienced what is like to live on Earth, or what is like to have a family that cares for you and loves you unconditionally. You've never felt what is like to have friends and be free, to live a peaceful life and be human for once," I explained.

"What is it like?" she asked, interested.

"What is what like?"

"To be human?"

"It's beautiful! You live life to the fullest, explore its wonders and the beauty of nature. You learn the difference between love, pain, joy and hate. Most importantly, you learn to live. Being human has its own disadvantages too though. You go through tough situations, and sometimes make bad decisions that you later regret, yet you learn from your mistakes, which makes you a better person as you grow. Not to mention, you don't get to live forever, but at least you take those great moments and memories with you for all eternity after you die. For me, I think that's what matters the most."

"So family is very important to you." She paused for a minute. "What is it like to be loved?"

She made me smile.

"Why do you want to know?" I asked.

"I was just—I was wondering—what's so great about your world for you to do what you just did?" she said embarrassed. She got serious again. "I heard there is an army somewhere in the city," she informed me.

"Yeah, the Satunians. I saw them marching somewhere in the city too. I don't know where they were headed though."

"Actually, it's your army."

I gasped. "My army?"

"Rukus and some of my cyclops have been spying on your army for quite awhile now."

"Who is that freak anyway?"

"It sounds like you've met before."

"Yeah, and he is not very nice."

"He's in charge of a portion of my territory. He reports to me," she said.

"Do you trust him?"

"No," was her simple reply. "I trust no demon."

"Oh! But me trusting you was an exception," I said with sarcasm.

"He must not know that I'm helping you. If he finds out, he'll turn my demons against me and tell Satu." There was a long pause. "Come with me," she said.

"Where are we going now?"

"I'm going to take you to the people you love. Your family."

An alarm was heard and the crowd started moving fast. They were all preparing themselves for something big.

"Why are they gearing up?" Craig asked, running towards Christine.

"The Satunians are moving in," she said.

"They're going to attack now? And start a war in the middle of the night?"

"You're talking about Satunians, Craig. They never play fair," Rebecca said, joining the conversation. She walked up to them with Nathan, Jack and Clara right behind her.

"You don't say!" Jack responded with sarcasm.

"We need to get our men and women ready. This might get ugly soon," Christine said.

"What can we do?" Nathan asked her.

"We wait."

"Aren't we gearing up too?" Craig asked.

"Guardians do not fight this battle."

Everyone looked at her, concerned.

"Christine? We can't just stand here and do nothing," Jack added.

"We must wait. It isn't our time yet."

The crowd started walking out through all the exits in the coliseum and marched uptown. They were all prepared and ready to fight for their future.

"How do we know when the time is right?" Craig asked.

"When The Chosen One gathers all his guardians. Erick will choose them at the right moment. I just hope he's okay."

"He is!" came a voice from behind.

A young man walked down to the middle of the arena. He was smiling.

Clara started tearing from joy. Everyone was happy to see

him. Clara ran to him first and hugged him tightly. Jack and Christine joined them too, and together they hugged from joy.

"I haven't seen you guys in years," Erick said, still hugging his parents. He didn't want to let go. "I thought I'd never see you again."

"It's okay, baby. We are here now." Clara said.

Erick knew he had forgotten how his parents looked like at one point. Just remembering those awful memories made him want to hug his parents even longer. Christine was relieved to know he was okay.

Erick was happy to see her too, but he was afraid she would ask about Harris. What could he possibly say? After all, it was his fault he was dead. She would never forgive him for that. He wasn't going to be able to hide the truth forever, but he decided not to talk about it until he felt it was the right moment.

Clara took a quick look at Erick for a few seconds. She realized he had changed drastically. He was a lot different. He looked more mature, taller, stronger, and tired. She hugged him again, realizing he had gone through a lot. She knew he must have been alone and lost all this time in the underworld.

She looked behind his shoulder and saw a demon.

"What is that?!" Clara shouted while pointing at Lola. Erick noticed Christine was heading for a gun.

"Wait! Hold on. It's alright. She's with me," he said quickly before his grandmother shot her.

"What is this demon doing here, Erick?" Christine asked.

"She's helping me."

"Helping you? You trust this demon?"

"I do. She's here because she wants the same thing we do. To defeat Satu," was his reply. Everyone looked at each other.

"It's true," Lola confirmed. "I've joined forces with Ethasus today, not because I want to, but because I have to. The Order cannot be destroyed."

Christine wasn't buying it, and the rest of the crew didn't feel comfortable with her joining the team either.

"Look. This is not about The Order anymore. This is about something far worse than that. Satu wants to become a devil. He wants all the power in the world and right now he's got the upper hand because—I… It… It's my fault."

"What happened, Erick?" Clara asked.

"The Others were captured," he mumbled. Everyone couldn't believe the news.

"How did this happen?" Christine asked.

"They tried to rescue me, but Pops… he…"

"Where's Harris?"

Erick was silent. He didn't know how to tell them.

"He's—"

"It was my idea," Lola finished. "I ambushed The Others because I had a plan. I asked Ethasus to join me, but everything got out of hand once Satu had control over them. He ordered one of them to kill his grandfather." Everyone stood quiet.

"That can't be." Christine broke the silence, not believing. Clara didn't buy it either. They were more confused than sad.

"It's true. He died in my arms. The Others were controlled by The Book of Mythos," Erick said with his voice cracking.

"If The Others are being controlled by black magic, then that means we can reverse the spell and get them back," Christine advised. Clara also agreed.

When Erick heard that, his face changed. It seemed as if not all was lost. Erick felt relieved. There was still hope to win this battle and get his friends back.

"Transformation won't work without Erick," Clara informed.

"Exactly!" Christine exclaimed. They all turned to Erick at the same time. Erick had no idea what they were talking about. He found it really strange that Christine and Clara weren't mourning for Harris. They ignored the fact he was gone and went back to business. He thought that's how dedicated his guardians were.

"Craig? What's the status?" Christine asked.

"Our army is in position," Craig informed them while listening to a radio transmission with his headphones on. "The

Satunians started attacking our front liners. They are coming at them by numbers, and…" he paused for a second.

"—Oh no!"

"What's wrong? What's happening?" she asked.

"They have demons."

"What?!" Erick uttered. He glanced at Lola. Lola wasn't aware of that either.

"You said your demons weren't going to attack my people," Erick questioned.

"My demons are not attacking your people," she reassured. She was very much confused as well.

"Then who is?" Erick shouted.

Lola thought about it for a second. She didn't have an answer.

"Do you think Rukus knows about us?" he asked, pacing back and forth.

"It's possible, but I doubt he has something to do with this."

"It has to be him," Erick said, a bit anxious. "You have to do something, Lola."

"I'll see what I can do," Lola said, and ran out the nearest exit and flew off.

Erick was idle for a minute. He had a lot on his mind. He knew the war had started. He knew this was the beginning of what could be the end. He knew he had to gather all his guardians and fight with everything he had. If his grandmother was right about The Book of Mythos, then he might have a chance. If not, he would have to seek help from Orcoptu. But that would only mean selling his soul.

He turned slowly to his guardians.

"It is time," he asserted. Then he turned to Nathan and Rebecca. "You started this," Erick addressed them with a serious tone of voice. "Now it's time for you to fix it." They were all tensed. He turned to everyone and spoke again. "You will all join me today as guardians and fight with me until the end."

Nathan and Rebecca were shocked that Erick would even choose them as his guardians to begin with.

"Our priority right now is to get The Book of Mythos. Without The Others, we don't stand a chance." He looked back at Rebecca. "I need you to get the book for me."

She didn't argue. She had no other choice. She knew what she did. All of this happened because of her personal vendetta against the guardians. But now she was a guardian herself and she had a chance to fix things. It was her responsibility.

She walked up to a table that was filled with ammunition and all types of weaponry and grabbed a 9mm and a few magazines. She locked and loaded then looked at Erick as a sign she was ready.

"Where is Satu?" Rebecca asked, eager to know.

She and Satu had a score to settle. This was not about helping him conquer the world anymore. This was about making him pay for what he did. She put her life on the line for him, and she believed in his cause. All for nothing. The many years she spent trying to get him out of Inferno got her wanting to kick him back into the hell he came from.

"I need you to go with her," Erick said, looking at Nathan.

He nodded.

Erick told them about the museum, and where he last saw the book. As they were ready to leave, Erick called out to them one last time.

"Guys?" They both turned to him. "I understand we need The Others back, but you are my guardians now and your lives are as important to me. So don't go Rambo out there and stay safe, alright? If things get out of hand, just forget about the book, and join the rest of us here, okay?" Nathan and Rebecca were happy to know that The Chosen One didn't hate them for what they did. He had given them a second chance to make things right. They weren't going to screw this one up again. They both left the arena in search of the book.

"What should we do now, Erick?" Craig asked.

Erick turned to him.

"We're going to join my army and finish this."

The Satunians and the Detarrunian army were battling each other to the death. The Detarrunians had the upper hand at first. They used all their militia and weapons against the Satunians.

Until the demons arrived.

These demons were different. They weren't like the cyclops. They were bigger, and more powerful. They destroyed their tanks and slaughtered many by numbers. They ripped the Detarrunians' bodies apart, slit their throats with their nails and chewed off their heads with their humongous mouths. There was a lot of bloodshed in Downtown Manhattan.

It was a horrifying sight.

The more people they massacred, the more the Satunians cheered. They were wicked, and they were winning this war.

When Erick first got to the battlefield and witnessed such things for himself, it simply pained him so much. He didn't expect to see such cruelty and violence against his people. He had to witness many amputees slithering away from the carnage, legs and hands scattered around the streets and so many people dying in the most horrifying ways, right before his eyes.

What pained him most was that he couldn't do anything about it. Erick's rage for Satu grew stronger by the minute. He swore he was going to make him pay for this.

None of his guardians expected to see this carnage either. They were all hiding near a building close by. From there, they were able observe what was happening in the battlefield first hand.

Erick had the impulse to run and join his army, but Clara held him back, shaking her head lightly.

"We must wait until we have the book," she reminded him calmly.

"I hope they get to the book before it's too late," Christine said.

"What happens after we get the book?" Craig asked.

"We kill Satu and his entire army," Erick replied, enraged. He was pacing back and forth. Everyone noted that he was not in the mood, and he surely wasn't the same Erick they used to know.

This Erick had changed. The entire world was counting on him, which was a serious responsibility for a teenager. He seemed more and more agitated.

They didn't blame him for being so angry either. Anyone else would have given up a long time ago, or gone mental. All this time he had done an amazing job handling every situation accordingly, but just how much could he take? He was only human, and he was only 16.

There is only so much one can take before they break.

The Metropolitan Museum of Arts

"This is the room Erick was talking about," Rebecca whispered. She and Nathan managed to sneak inside the museum unnoticed.

They approached a door in the middle of a hallway.

"Are you sure this is the one?" Nathan asked. His heart was beating fast and he knew that Satu could be anywhere in these rooms. He also knew what he was capable of. The odds of running into him were 99% out of 100%. Just the thought of that made him tremble in fear.

"Come on," Rebecca said. She opened the door just enough to peek inside. The room was empty. No Satunians or demons. Together, they stepped in the room.

The room was big just as Erick described it, with a dome in the ceiling. They both searched the place, but there was no sign of the book.

"Satu must have it," Nathan said. "Definitely not gonna leave it out of his sight either."

"We can't go back without it," she insisted.

They heard voices coming from the room next door. They stood quiet and got closer to the walls, and listened carefully.

"You are killing the humans!"

"Yes... Yes... For power..."

"Those are not my demons."

Nathan and Rebecca recognized those voices. It was Satu and Lola. What they heard was unexpected. Things were escalating into a different level.

"We really need to find that book, Nathan!" Rebecca said desperately.

"Looking for this?" came a voice from behind them.

They turned startled, and saw Oliver the messenger holding the book in his hands. He stared awkwardly at them.

"What are you doing here?" he asked.

"We are here for the book, and I'm not afraid to use this," Rebecca warned, pointing her gun at Oliver.

He didn't flinch. Instead, he turned his back to them.

"You really think that's going to help you?" he asked roguishly.

"I'll take my chances, now give us the book," she ordered.

"You humans never learn." He turned back to face them, jumped up in the air and transformed into a giant half human and half bat creature. He hovered in the air with his big bat wings, and holding on to the book, taunted them.

"Come and get it, if you can." He snickered.

Rebecca knew that if she used her gun, it would alert Satu and his army. They couldn't risk doing that. Nathan scanned the room for something to use against Oliver. Rebecca did too. Desperately, they both found something.

Oliver came at them flying and they both dodged out of the way. Nathan used a chair and threw it at him, but missed. Oliver chased him around the room.

Rebecca quickly used an old sword that was on display on the wall and swung the thing at Oliver. He was so focused on Nathan, he didn't realize she had cut off his left wing.

Oliver dropped the book and tended his wounded wing. Rebecca tried to strike again but he grabbed her arm, and squeezed her hand, hard. She let go of the sword from the pain. She thought she might lose that hand for sure.

"Quick, Nathan! Get the book!" Rebecca shouted frantically.

It was like a slow motion movie.

It was perfect timing for Nathan. He jumped across the room where Oliver had dropped the book, fell on his stomach, reached out, grabbed it and rolled out of the way. Oliver saw he had the book now, so he let go of Rebecca's hand and turned to him.

Huge mistake.

"Psssst."

Oliver turned back to her. Little did he know that she was ready for him. All he saw was the cylinder from the tip of her gun, before she pulled the trigger and shot him square in the head.

He dropped dead instantly. That alerted the Satunians in the building.

"Let's get out of here, hurry!" Nathan shouted. When they opened the door to leave the room, they came face to face with another demon.

"Lola?" Nathan exclaimed, not expecting to see her there.

She pushed them back into the room, grabbed them both and flew them out through the glass ceiling.

CHAPTER 19

THE PACT

"THIS IS GETTING OUT of hand. I can't just hide back here and watch!" I yelled.

Rebecca and Nathan weren't back with the book yet and my army was being slaughtered by the minute.

"We need to be patient, Erick," Dad said.

"I need to help my people, Dad," I disputed. "They can't fight this war alone."

"We've been spotted!" my grandmother screamed, as she pointed at a giant demon heading our way.

"Run! Get out of here!" I screamed.

"We are not leaving you," Mom said.

"I've already lost one guardian and I'm not losing another, so get out of here now. It's an order," I commanded. I wasn't playing around and I was totally serious. She didn't expect that out of me either, but she got the point. She knew we couldn't jeopardize our mission.

"You heard him, let's go," she instructed the rest of the team. They all ran the opposite direction towards a nearby building.

I waited for this giant to get closer. This one didn't have any wings, horns, or one eye like Lola's cyclops. This was a different type of demon. It had long arms and legs, skull-like features, and was very skinny. He had long nails and long sharp teeth. It looked more like Hollows. His body looked burnt, sort of how human bodies look after a 3rd degree burn. It was really horrific. His eyes weren't human and they stared at me abnormally.

"Alright, ugly, what's your weakness?" I asked the thing. Cyclops had a weakness and it was the eyes. What about this one?

I saw something move from the corner of my right eye. It was another one of those things. As I moved back, another jumped off the roof of a nearby building and landed a few feet behind me.

Crap! I was surrounded. This is not what I had in mind.

The first demon growled at me and ran towards me. I rolled out of the way, and heard the one behind me coming. I turned quickly and kicked him on the jaw. He howled loudly. The other two blocked my way out, so I ran the other direction, straight into the battlefield, where it was swarming with more of these ugly things.

I kept running, thinking I would probably lose them through the crowd.

That's what I thought.

Somehow, as I ran through the crowd of Satunians and Detarrunians, I attracted everyone's attention. What the heck were they looking at?

The other three demons were gaining on me. I tried to speed up, but accidentally tripped on a dead body and fell to the ground, on my stomach. That was actually the worst thing that could've happened.

The first demon jumped on my back, then the other two tried to attack me as well. All I could do was use my arms as shield. Fortunately for me, a group of military men started firing at the demons with G36s and MK46 machine guns.

They got them off my back.

Other demons and Satunians were heading towards me now.

The soldiers helped me up and tactically covered me from danger while they fired their guns. Together, we made it to the center of the battlefield where the Satunians and demons had my army surrounded.

"Make way, make way!" one of the soldiers yelled. He was the lieutenant in command of his team.

The demons started attacking our circle and the Satunians were shooting at us too. One of the soldiers who rescued me was shot in the shoulder. He landed on his back, hurt.

"Justin?" The lieutenant yelled. He came and helped him up as he kept shooting.

We couldn't hold them back any longer.

A demon jumped high up in the air and landed on top of me inside of our circle. I tried to protect myself. He bit my arm and cut me in the stomach with his claws. I thought he had ripped right through my intestines; thankfully, he didn't, but it still hurt so much. The other soldiers started shooting at it, but it kept biting my arm and he refused to die. I was in pretty bad shape already and I couldn't take the pain.

The lieutenant came running, pulled out a knife and slit the demon's throat, and got him off me.

"Don't worry, kid, we've got your back."

Another demon unexpectedly attacked him from behind, and ripped off his right hand.

It was too much for me to bear.

I was not going to let him die like this. He had saved my life twice, and it was time for me to return the favor. I had to make a decision for the sake of my people and the whole world.

I made up my mind and called out his name.

"ORCOPTU!"

A few seconds later, there were voices, diabolical voices that echoed all around us.

Every demon in the battle zone stopped attacking and just stared blankly.

The demons had fear in their eyes. They backed away slowly. I sat up and stared chaotically at what was happening. The demon that was attacking the Lieutenant bellowed loudly for all the other demons to hear. They started retreating.

Everyone stopped attacking each other and listened. There

was silence in the middle of the city. Then the ground started shaking under our feet. Nearby buildings began to collapse and the bright full moon turned red.

Something macabre was about to happen.

I was quivering and I didn't know why. I was scared for what would be the outcome of this. I'd never dealt with something of this magnitude before. I feared for my people and my life. What in Christ name did I let loose? I just released something from the darkest recesses of Hell. I wasn't even sure if what I did was the right thing to do. There was only one way to find out.

Then it happened.

"You hear that?" Justin asked.

Everyone was standing still. No one moved a muscle. There was a hissing sound and it was getting closer and louder. The demons started freaking out and ran away, but it was too late for them. Something dark and mystical appeared before them and it was cryptic and satanic. Something I can't explain because I'd never seen anything like it before.

We could all hear it.

It was Death in a form of a whisper. It was deadly, and it was killing them all. One by one, they started dying right before our eyes. It was like their souls were taken by something supernatural. Thousands of dead demons unexplainably collapsed to the ground dead. It was like a wave of bodies landing at our feet.

A few minutes later, my whole army of Detarrunians started cheering and shouting as a form of victory. I kinda did myself for a second too. I was relieved I was able to save some lives and I was able to help my people fight this war, but it was still far from over yet. I got on my feet slowly. I still had to lead my people through this war.

The Satunians, realizing they didn't have their demons anymore, started attacking us again. The war carried on where it left off. Even without their demons, the Satunians still had the upper hand and were not stopping.

We did lose a lot of my men and women on that first attack,

and this was just the beginning. I picked up a gun from a dead Satunian and with the little energy I had left, I started fighting side by side with my army.

Downtown Manhattan

"We need to stop," Rebecca commanded.

"We can't stop now," Lola said, still holding both of them, while she swooped them over the city away from danger.

"We need to reverse the curse. If we don't do it now, it will be too late," she urged.

Lola slowly descended close to the battlefield.

When they touched ground, Nathan and Rebecca were both disturbed at such a scene. They saw dead bodies everywhere. They weren't expecting this war to turn out so violent. Nathan felt so appalled, and at one point, he just couldn't breathe.

"What happened here?" Rebecca said almost in a whisper.

"It is already too late," Lola said.

"Why would you say that?" Nathan asked, upset.

"Look! Do you see that?" Lola replied, pointing at the moon. "It's red!"

"What does it mean?" Rebecca asked.

"It means Ethasus has sacrificed himself already."

"I'm still not understanding?" Nathan uttered.

"Satu was going to get to The Others no matter what. Instead of wasting time trying to get them back, I thought of a better idea. I offered Ethasus a different alternative."

"What did you do?" Rebecca asked, not trusting her.

"He asked a devil called Orcoptu to join him," Lola continued.

"And what will he get in return?" She clinched her teeth, not wanting to know.

"If Orcoptu helps him in battle, Ethasus has to sell his soul."

"Oh no, tell me he didn't?" Nathan asked, dazed.

"He did," was Lola's cold answer.

"Why would you take him there? I thought you were helping him?" he asked furiously.

"I am. I will help him through this till the end. It is why it was necessary. It had to be done," she said.

"What more would you expect from a demon?" Rebecca said angrily.

"Let's not forget who started this, and for what reasons," Lola challenged.

Rebecca didn't have a comeback for that one. Lola was right.

"Let's reverse the curse and end this war, once and for all," Nathan implored.

They all agreed.

Rebecca opened the book. She skipped through the black pages but she wasn't finding the page she was looking for. She was getting desperate.

"We overheard a conversation at the museum. It was a conversation between you and Satu. Please tell us it isn't true?" Nathan asked as his voice saddened.

Lola took a moment to answer.

"It's true," she replied. "The more people he kills, the more powerful he'll become. By the look of things, your whole army has been completely wiped out in just hours. Imagine how much power he will gain from another attack like this."

"Are The Others able to defeat him?"

"There is no doubt about that, but as I said before, Ethasus already sold his soul to Orcoptu. He belongs in the underworld now."

Such information had both of them worried.

"We'll get him back. For sure, The Others will too!"

"It'll be futile. Once a soul belongs to a devil, no one is able to get it back, not even archangels."

"I'm sure The Creator will not allow this," Nathan insisted.

"You are right, but remember, The Chosen One made his own choice."

Nathan stood there silent and wondering how devastated his parents would be once they heard about this.

"So this is it? It's over?" he said, feeling defeated.

"No, it's far from over, but this is where it gets complicated," Lola added. They both looked up, wanting to know more.

"What's the plan?"

"If Ethasus' soul is worth a lot in the underworld, imagine how much Satu's soul is worth now."

"So you're thinking a trade for a trade?" Rebecca asked.

"Exactly! But Satu will have to—" Lola didn't finish.

"Traitor!" came a roaring voice from the top of a five-story building.

"Run, get out of here. Reverse the curse and save your world!" Lola bellowed.

Nathan and Rebecca ran as far away from there as possible. Rukus jumped at Lola and attacked her and Lola counter attacked. Two powerful demons were about to clash. They were going to fight each other till the end.

Nathan and Rebecca wanted to help, but they had a mission to complete and they were going to do everything they could to make it happen.

"I found the page!" Rebecca said relieved, as they were still running.

The Battle

It was almost dawn.

I had pretty courageous men and women fighting by my side and they fought bravely. The Satunians were falling back little by little, and their numbers were decreasing. That was a good sign.

Throughout the whole night, I felt an evil presence close by. Something dark. I kept seeing it out of the corner of my eye, but when I looked, there was nothing there. Its power was immense and I felt it inside of me, like a sixth sense. It wasn't human either.

I thought maybe it was Orcoptu, taking over my body and

soul, but it wasn't a possession. It was a weird phenomenon, which kept watching my every move.

I felt a cold breeze in the back of my neck.

"Booo," came a male voice from behind.

Before I even had a chance to turn or look back, it was over. He got close to me and stabbed me right in my stomach with his sword. The unexpected blow had me feeling disoriented for a minute. I couldn't move or blink.

"I told you I wouldn't let you win," he said in my ear. He held me tightly with his other arm, pushing me towards the end of the sword, and used the other to push it deeper inside. He pulled the sword out, with an unmerciful force, just to rip through other tissues in my body. Blood came out of my mouth.

The pain was excruciating. I fell to the ground on my knees and took a quick look at my wound. There was a lot of blood. I was bleeding to death and I felt nauseous, cold and dizzy. I looked up at my opponent but I wish I hadn't.

I saw him licking my blood off the sword. He smiled at me, enjoying that. "You should've minded your own business, Ethasus. You of all people should have known better. Pains me really, that it ended this way. You and I could've ruled the world together. I might be an ambitious man, but I respect those who are loyal to me."

"You are nothing but a coward, you demented freak," I said, coughing out blood. I knew deep inside I was dying and there was nothing I could do. Still, I wasn't going to go down without a fight.

"Oh? You don't say," he mocked.

"That was a foul move, gotta give it to ya. You got me alright. It's a shame though, that a kid my age will make you go to these extremes. I bet you were desperate?" I teased back. His smirk disappeared.

He frowned at me with intensity. I think he was offended. He leaned closer to my face, stared me down for a few seconds, making me wait for his response.

"At least I didn't sell my soul to a devil," he answered with a smirk.

My whole world collapsed. Even the hair on the back of my neck stood up. How in the world could he have possibly have known that?

"Do you think I'm stupid? I knew all about you and Lola. It was just too obvious. As soon as Lola showed some type of interest in you, I had her own demons spy on her. That's when I heard she took you to see Orcoptu. It's a shame you would do something like that, Ethasus. Your grandfather will be so disappointed," he teased again.

I got so angry at him. I got on my feet fast, forgot about the pain and the blood I was losing quickly. I swung at him but missed. I kept swinging as he kept dodging all my punches. I started getting dizzy again and I fell to the ground. As I lay on my back, my whole body felt completely numbed. I couldn't move anymore.

I could even hear my own heartbeat.

I saw Satu hovering over me. He was standing there, gazing down at me. Watching my agonizing death.

"Farewell, my dear friend," he finally said. "Once I become a devil, I promise I'll pay you a visit in Hell, and maybe torture you some more." He laughed at me, then started walking away.

I picked up the sword he used against me with the little energy I still had left, stood up, and quickly ran to him. He never saw it coming.

I stabbed him in the back.

His head turned slowly. Even on that side angle, I could still feel his cold stare. He was furious. While he still glared at me, he slowly removed the sword from his back. It didn't even hurt him. He didn't even bleed.

"It seems I made a mistake." He said, "I should've put you out of your misery."

I backed away slowly. I knew what was coming, and it was going to hurt.

I ran.

Dying or not, I wasn't going to let him kill me. I kept stumbling over dead bodies, but I kept moving. I kept looking back to see if he was gaining on me.

I didn't see him anymore.

He had disappeared. I looked everywhere, prepared for whatever. I scanned through the crowd of Satunians and Detarrunians, who were still fighting each other. He was gone.

I kept running and tried to find my guardians. I got two blocks away when he reappeared right in front of me.

He grabbed me by the throat and punched me right on my wound. I cried in pain. He pummeled me over and over.

If he wanted to punish me, he sure was doing a heck of a job.

"I'm going to beat you so hard, you're going to beg me to kill you," he hissed. He let go of my neck and kneed me right in my chin. My head was spinning after that. He pushed me to the ground with a front kick and I accidently hurt my wound again.

Dang it.

He kept kicking me in the stomach while I was down. I couldn't breathe. I tried to get up on my feet every time, but I couldn't take the beating any longer. I couldn't even see straight. I didn't feel anything anymore. I was too dizzy and instead of fighting it, I just stayed on the ground.

I felt a strong arm wrap around my neck from behind. Satu had me in a headlock and he was choking me.

"Give up," he said.

"No."

He squeezed tighter. "I said, give up."

I felt these powerful beings. It was an amazing energy that surrounded me. I slowly turned my head to see where that energy was coming from. I looked straight ahead. Still trying to breathe and almost passing out, I tried my best to focus on the figures in front of me.

I recognized them.

They were my archangels. They were different now and they looked stronger. They were back!

Next to them were my guardians, all seven of them, and they were ready. Clara, Jack, Craig, Christine, Nathan, and Rebecca and most importantly, my grandfather Harris. He was still alive. Kate, Sarah and Matheus were amongst them too.

My soul wasn't hurting any longer and I was filled with joy.

My grandfather nodded. It was a sign, and somehow I understood what it meant. It was time to end this.

"I was chosen by The Creator," I spoke, gasping for air. "I was chosen to save the world, and to protect The Order." I got on one knee. "That's what I was born to do, and that's exactly what I will do. I won't let you win, and I'm definitely not giving up." I don't know how this incredible energy came over me. It was enough to lift him off the ground and throw him over my shoulder. He landed on his back, right in front of me. He backed away from me with his eyes widened. He watched me, mystified. He couldn't comprehend how I did that.

I couldn't either.

This was new to me. I didn't feel pain anymore. I felt new and stronger.

CHAPTER 20

THE FINAL BATTLE

I WAS STANDING TALL after that beat down and the sword wound Satu had given me.

Satu got on his feet still puzzled.

My archangels joined me and surrounded him. He was so fixated in torturing me that he never realized my allies were there all along. He still thought he had them under control.

"Kill him," he commanded.

They all had mean expressions on their faces. I could only imagine what they were thinking. "I suggest you come forth before The Creator, and face the consequences of your actions," Larry declared.

He did not take that very lightly. He erupted with anger, and started pulling the skin off his head. His madness turned him into a malignant and ferocious goblin who would destroy anything in its path. He came at us fast.

Luis grabbed me quickly and moved me away from him, but he was determined to stop me from defeating him. He turned to my guardians.

Oh no.

The Others noted his intentions and ran quickly towards him. Jimmy punched him on the head while Patrick held the beast by its neckline. Satu countered the attack with his powerful fist, and almost got Larry, but Larry was way faster than him. These guys kept hitting him harder and harder but nothing seemed to stop him.

He was absorbing every hit like a cushion.

He was so fast he left a trail of particles behind. Together the boys attacked full force. At one point, Jimmy and Bruce both struck at their target, making him fly up a few feet in the air like a missile. Then Luis prodded him down to the floor.

There was a big bang heard all across the city. There was a huge crater left from the attack. It was so powerful Satu's body was twisted in an impossible position, the Exorcism way.

He was on the ground, his face facing up and his torso was backwards. It was an atrocious sight. His body was twitching from that blow. I thought for sure it was over, but this beast was just getting warmed up. His face turned and faced me with a bloody smirk. I watched in horror as his eyes were now fixed on mine. I didn't want to be anywhere near that thing.

With his head still looking at me, he got up and started stalking me. The image was disturbing. He forced his body back to its correct position and I only heard his bones crack during the process.

I wanted to puke.

It was as if nothing had happened. Even the guys couldn't believe he was still moving. Luis jolted Satu hard again and he landed on top of a building somewhere.

He came back for more. The boys attacked together, one at a time. It was something out of this world. It was one of the coolest things I'd ever witnessed in my life.

Satu looked hurt but the beating was not enough to take him down for good.

He stopped attacking and started laughing out loud. The guys stared back in confusion.

Then his skin tone started changing and his body shape as well. He was transforming into something horrendous and hideous. Long horns came out of his forehead, his back, chin, and shoulder blades. His teeth sharpened as well as his nails. His clothes ripped apart when muscles like the Incredible Hulk appeared. He mutated into something hellish and satanic. He roared loudly. His voice was different and distorted too.

We all stared awkwardly, as this creature changed before our eyes. All this time we had been killing demons, but nothing like this one.

Still, every demon had a weakness.

Bruce and Patrick attacked the new Satu. If he wasn't going down in his regular form, he sure wasn't going down now. Every attack from the boys was useless. The rest of them joined too, but they were no match.

They retreated fast. They realized that none of their close range attacks were working with his new transformation.

He surprisingly stuck his tongue out, elongating it and reached out to Jimmy's neck. He pulled and squeezed tighter, trying to break his neck. In just a blink of an eye, Satu's tongue was cut in half. I couldn't believe Luis did that with just a simple hand movement. That only made Satu angrier. He came at Luis, and was so fast even Luis didn't see it coming. He grabbed him by his hair and slammed his head onto the concrete floor. We all thought he was dead after an injury like that.

"Luis?" I called worried.

Larry attacked him from behind, trying to keep him away from Luis. Satu unexpectedly caught Larry by his shirt, then opened his mouth and bit him on the neck. He started sucking his blood.

THIS WAS INSANE!

Jimmy, Patrick and Bruce tried to save him, but he didn't let go of Larry.

"You're killing him!" I yelled.

Larry kicked and elbowed him, trying to get him off, but Satu was a giant leech, sucking all the blood out of him and he wasn't letting go.

Surprisingly, he did let go of Larry.

When he did, he ripped off a chunk of Larry's neck. He collapsed to the floor, in pain and bleeding.

"No, Larry!" I screamed.

Satu was looking for his next target. He spotted just the guy. He was coming for me again. He ran towards me like a bull and pointed those sharp horns my way.

Jimmy got in the way, trying to protect me, but Satu's horns penetrated right through his skin.

He flung him off his horns up in the air and Jimmy landed a few feet away severely injured.

A huge hand came at me fast. Satu now had me by the neck. He squeezed hard and flung me down to the ground with force. As I was on the ground, he placed his giant foot on my chest pinning me to the ground so I wouldn't be able to get away. His foot was heavy too. He looked up at my guardians and then at my archangels, searching for another challenger.

Patrick came at him full speed. He thought he had him but Satu's hands ripped right through his chest.

"No!" I cried.

Patrick's blood splattered all over as Satu held him in the air dangling from his arm. When Satu removed his arm from his chest, Patrick collapsed to the ground not moving.

He was cruel. I couldn't watch any more.

My archangels were going to get killed if I didn't think of something.

I glanced at my guardians. I needed their guidance once more. They knew what I was going to do. They all held hands and closed their eyes. My grandfather got The Book of Mythos from Rebecca; he opened it, and started reading the ancient Detarrunian language. Whatever he was saying, it was magical.

As I lay under Satu's foot, I decided to close my eyes, while I took deep breaths and listened very carefully. Listened carefully to my soul. I needed to know what I was supposed to do. I needed to know how to save the world, and I needed that guidance now. The concentration was a hard process. But I had to concentrate.

Satu turned back to me and was about to grab me but he stopped.

He felt something. He felt the power within me. He removed his foot from my chest and backed away slowly. He knew exactly what was coming.

I felt electricity running through my veins. I blacked out and lost control of my body.

The sky turned dark.

There was wind blowing 60 miles per hour and a thunderstorm was developing.

Satu tried to attack me again, but something pushed him back, almost knocking him off his feet. It was a shield I unconsciously created within me. Then involuntarily, I started speaking another language.

It was Detarrunian.

"Fuse," I said in a soft voice.

My archangels started glowing, and were generating an enormous amount of energy. It was some kind of celestial power that was being transmitted through all of us.

I kept my eyes closed, and was in a deep meditative state. While I focused and listened very carefully, I felt seven different energies activating within my body. Each one provided me with Divine Purpose, Intuition, Judgment, Compassion, Emotional Balance, Creativity, and Stability.

I heard a dog barking in the distance.

Matheus ran towards me and transformed into a metal object. While Matheus was still transforming, The Others started floating up in the air. They were suspended off the ground and they started shining an incredible white light.

Matheus and the archangels disappeared into thin air.

This was the transformation Satu feared. He tried to stop it, but my shield impeded him from touching me.

The Others reappeared in the form of light. The light possessed my body and soul.

I thought my heart had stopped and the light hurt my body,

but my wounds were healed. I was changing every second into something else. Matheus now appeared in the form of a golden heavenly sword.

I finally opened my eyes, and grabbed the sword in my hand.

This was the moment to make things right. I had finally accepted my destiny and most importantly, I accepted who I was.

"I am Ethasus, and I'm finally ready."

THE CHOSEN ONE

It was morning in New York City, and the sun was rising.

Once everybody in the city saw Erick transforming, they stopped fighting each other and watched in wonder. They couldn't believe the amount of energy this young boy had.

The Others and Matheus were now a part of Erick, and Erick was now a part of them. They fused into something different. United as one, they changed him and he wasn't human anymore.

He was an angelic celestial being with incredible powers.

White wings spread across his back. They were about 12 feet long and he had Detarrunian tribal markings tattooed all over his back and arms. They were the symbols of Heaven, Paradise, Earth, Purgatory, Inferno and Hell. The six realms he was chosen to protect.

He was the guardian angel of both humanity and the underworld.

Satu growled at Erick, enraged. He ran to him and went for the kill.

Erick didn't move.

He didn't even flinch. In fact, he looked straight into the beast's eyes, as he waited patiently for the attack. Just when Satu thought he had him, he didn't.

He saw him standing on the same spot as if he never moved out of the way.

He was invincible.

Satu side kicked him, but Erick caught his foot midair, with his left hand. Satu almost had him by an inch. He slowly shoved him, and Satu fell backwards a few yards away, leaving a trail. Now moving faster than light, he came at Satu full throttle with his golden sword. He ran by him so quickly in a zig zag, there was only a blur.

The guardians watched in awe in the distance.

Erick stood behind him, with his back to him.

Satu tried to attack, but he realized something was wrong.

Both his arms and legs fell off. Blood spilled like a sprinkler valve. He collapsed on his face with no limbs to break the fall. His mouth and eyes were wide open in shock. He lifted his head to look up at Erick slowly.

"It can't be, I'm way stronger than you, how did you—" He choked on his own blood.

Erick now looking down at him said these simple words, "Life is beautiful. It's full of love, and it's full of life. It isn't fair, that you drag others to their deaths and misery, just because you have chosen that path. You are no devil and neither will you be a god."

Satu hesitated to answer. He took a second to think about his response.

"You are all worthless. You were all born to serve me and die. You will not win this war, Ethasus."

Erick was about to walk away when Satu called out. "I summon you, Orcoptu."

Erick turned to him. He could not believe he would do this now.

"Orcoptu? I want more power and immortality. Let me become the devil The Chosen One so intends to stop me from becoming and in return, I will trade my soul for his!" He shouted proudly, still choking on his own blood. He started laughing hysterically. He believed he had won. He believed he had the upper hand.

"As you wish," came a sinister voice from behind Erick.

It was Orcoptu himself. He appeared in the air transparently, but enough to know he was there.

Orcoptu grabbed him by the back of his neck.

"Wait!" Satu screamed, realizing what was going on. "What are you doing?"

They disappeared instantly in midair, leaving his limbs behind. The only thing that was heard were his echoing screams, while he disappeared forever and taken to Hell, where he would be shackled for all eternity. Like the rest of the devils.

"A trade for a trade. Just as Lola predicted," Erick said in a whisper.

His wings disappeared and so did his powers. A few seconds later, he fainted. His guardians ran to him.

Clara and Jack got to him first, but Erick wasn't moving. He appeared to be in a coma.

"He's not breathing!" Clara screamed as she looked for a pulse. "Somebody help him!" she cried.

Erick started glowing again.

A colorful light left his body and his sword. The light transformed into five human beings. The Others.

They went back to their original human forms, and so did Matheus. They all regained consciousness and looked at each other oddly. They realized their wounds were gone too. They saw Erick was not okay and ran towards him.

"Erick?" Larry shouted. He examined him for a second "What's happening? Why isn't he breathing?"

"I don't know. He's not waking up," Clara cried. Jack hugged her tightly. He had fear in his eyes. Fear of losing his son again.

"Stay back, give him room to breathe!" Kate shouted as she ran as fast as she could.

She immediately performed CPR on him. She did the 30 pumps and 2 breaths routine for about a minute, but there was still no sign of life. Kate was afraid she might have gotten there too late. She started getting anxious.

"You are not going to die on me, not today, you hear me?" She tilted his head back, pinched his nose and blew air one last time.

Erick started coughing.

Kate and Clara were relieved and smiling with happiness. Erick was slowly starting to breathe again at last. He opened his eyes and looked around. The first thing he saw were two beautiful blue eyes.

"Erick? Are you okay?" Kate asked.

Erick looked at her, then saw Sarah, his guardians, Matheus and his archangels waiting on him to respond. He gave them a weak smile.

"I'm okay. What happened?" he asked, disoriented.

"You don't remember?" Jimmy asked. He shook his head. "Dude! You kicked butt!"

Erick stood up gently. His parents and his grandparents hugged him tightly. He hugged them back too. "I'm so proud of you," Jack said. Erick smiled at him then looked at his grandfather.

"Pops? I thought you were dead," Erick said.

"Of course not. I'm a guardian remember? Guardians don't die," Harris responded.

"Oh! Right," he replied, embarrassed. He got on his feet, Larry and Jack helped him up.

He turned back to Kate.

"Thank you, Kate. I owe you my life."

"Don't mention it," she said smiling. He hugged her tightly, and she hugged back. It was a magical moment for him. He wanted to kiss her but didn't dare. Everybody was watching them. When he let go he started blushing. She was blushing too.

He looked around, and saw that Earth was saved once more, and so was The Order. Nothing made him happier.

There was a clear blue sky in Downtown Manhattan and the war was finally over between the Satunians and the Detarrunians.

There was finally peace once more.

A lot of lives were lost that night, but because of the fallen and their valiant acts, a billion other lives were saved all around the world.

"Mom?" a man called.

There were four soldiers walking towards Erick. Two of them looked familiar to him. It was Justin and the lieutenant who saved him in the battlefield.

"Chris?" Sarah called, crying. She ran to the lieutenant and they hugged. They were both crying with joy.

Matheus smelled a familiar scent. He knew who it was and he was thrilled to see him again. As soon as he saw Matt in the distance, Matheus ran to him and jumped all on him licking his face.

"There you are, Milo! I was looking all over for you. Where have you been?" Matt said, happy to see him. Matheus just kept wagging his tail and licking his face.

Kate's parents were also amongst the crowd. So were Jimmy's, Bruce's, Luis' and Patrick's. Everyone was reunited with their loved ones.

Erick looked at each and every one of his guardians and noticed that Rebecca and Nathan were in the back, not being acknowledged. He walked over to them and hugged them too.

"Thank you," Erick said.

"For what?" Nathan asked.

"For fighting by my side till the end." They both smiled back at him, pleased to hear him say that. They were also welcomed by the rest of the team a few seconds later. He knew there was someone else missing.

He searched around for her. He walked behind a building nearby and found her on the ground wounded pretty badly.

It was Lola. Erick ran to her and helped her sit up.

"What happened?"

"Rukus," she answered.

"Where is he?" Erick asked, ready to fight some more.

"He's dead..." He looked around and saw his dead body a few

feet away. "You... did it, Ethasus! You saved The Order and our worlds," she said, smiling slightly and coughing blood.

That was actually the first time he had ever seen her smile before.

"We need to treat your wounds. You're bleeding pretty bad." He was going to carry her but saw a fatal wound in her stomach and chest.

"Don't," she said stopping him. "I'm fine..."

"But you could die."

"If I do... at least... It was an honor... fighting with you," she said proudly.

"Lola?" Erick said with a sad voice. "I'm so sorry for not trusting you."

"I'm a demon. You're not supposed to."

"You knew all along. You knew Satu would do anything just to win."

Lola nodded.

Erick felt even guiltier for not trusting her.

"Why did you help me, Lola? Why betray your kind because of me?" Erick asked the injured demon in his arms. She looked at him for a minute then smiled again.

"I helped you because—" she coughed "—I wanted to know what it was like to be human for once," was her final answer fading away.

She slowly closed her eyes and wasn't breathing anymore. Erick's heart was filled with sadness.

He really liked Lola. It was tough for him to know she was gone. He wouldn't have made it this far if it wasn't for her. "No, Lola? Lola?" he cried as he called her name. He laid her lifeless body on the ground.

There was a moment of silence. Not only for Lola, but also for those who died during the war.

He saw a swarm of cyclops flying over the blue sky, retreating back to Inferno. Lola wasn't around anymore, so they all went back to their respective dimensions. Erick saw an immense crowd walking towards him and the team. It was his Detarrunian army and the Satunians.

They all gathered near The Chosen One. They all kneeled, showing respect to their young hero. He felt honored to have fought with such brave men and women. His guardians and The Others also got on one knee. It was an incredible feeling. For the first time, he was proud to be chosen.

"Thank you, everyone," Erick spoke. He looked at the multitude of people who were now looking up to him, and continued, "I truly believe you should all bow to one another. Everyone here played a big part in history. Because of you, Earth and The Order is saved. You stood up for what you truly believed in. You fought with everything you had, because you believed in something. You believed in life, love, and peace. You held on to that belief till the end. I can't even explain how important you guys are to me. You are the reason why I did what I did. Because I love each and every one of you. Satu or not, we are all human beings, we are all family, we are not perfect, and we definitely make mistakes. I know I made many, but because of those mistakes, I am here today. This is not the end. This is just the beginning. Let's pick ourselves up, and together, we'll make it right again," he finished.

Everyone cheered. Most of them were crying. Some shouted patriotically.

He looked at the crowd and noted some of these people didn't even have homes anymore. Some lost their families in the battle too.

Erick felt horrible. He deeply wanted to help. He wanted to change things. It occurred to him that maybe there could be a way. That perhaps he could. He felt the need to give it a try.

Besides, he literally went through hell just to save the world, so he deserved an explanation. He deserved some answers, and he definitely had some demands. He knew exactly where to go and who to ask.

He looked at Matheus. "Take me to Heaven," he ordered.

Clara and Christine were about to say something, but remained silent. Matheus didn't ask any questions either. He simply did as he was told. Matheus instantly transformed into the majestic phoenix he had rode on many times before. Erick jumped on Matheus' back, turned to the crowd and gave them a salute gesture. He made his way up in the sky with Matheus, until he was no longer seen anymore.

"What is he up to?" Jack asked Clara.

"He is on his way to see The Creator," Harris replied, smiling at him.

CHAPTER 21

HEAVEN

WHAT AN AMAZING WORLD. It was a city in the clouds. Never thought I would see The Gates to Heaven in the flesh. It was similar to Paradise in a way, but a lot richer in greatness. It was the perfect world for the gods.

As soon as we left my dimension, these white and long marbled floors appeared. They were huge and they led to these humongous gates that had a design of a sun in the middle, the symbol of light and perfection. Matheus told me that no one had ever stepped inside these gates before. Only the gods and The Creator were allowed in this realm.

But I didn't care. I had to try.

As soon as we got closer, I dismounted Matheus, and walked up to the gates. I studied them in wonder. The doors were made out of pure gold. I pushed the doors, but they were locked. I knocked as hard as I could and heard an echo from my knocks. Then there was a moment of silence.

I looked at Matheus who was also dazed staring at the doors. I knocked a few times again and no one answered. I sat there and waited for maybe two minutes. I turned disappointed and was ready to leave. As soon as I turned, they slowly opened up.

There was light, the brightest light I'd ever seen. I had to cover my eyes for a minute. After my eyes adjusted a little bit, I saw this figure in a white robe. He was tall and skinny. His skin was not white, nor black.

He was just perfect.

He had white hair and didn't have a beard.

He was very different.

"I was expecting you," the figure spoke. "I am The Creator, and you must be Ethasus!"

I went blank. I had so many questions to ask, yet there he was, standing in front of me and I couldn't think of anything to say.

"I know why you are here." He spoke again. "You are here because you need answers, and you have demands."

He kind of took the words out of my mouth.

"Please, come inside," he said as he welcomed me in.

"Why me?" I finally asked. I was a little shaken up.

This guy was THE GOD.

He stared at me, not believing I just asked that question. He walked past me, and with his back facing me, moved his right hand very gently to the side. I saw how a few clouds came apart, revealing the most magnificent and extraordinary view.

Five realms.

They were all aligned vertically, starting with Paradise, next my beautiful blue planet Earth, then Purgatory, Inferno and lastly, Hell. We were on the very top of all worlds, which was Heaven.

"Do you see those beautiful worlds?" he asked.

I was about to ask what was so great about Hell and Inferno, but when you saw them from this angle, they were the most spectacular perfect creations you've ever seen.

"Yes," I replied amazed.

"What do you see?"

I looked closely for a second. "Uh, I see that some worlds are good, but there are some that are evil."

"Exactly! The spirits that live in them make them what they are."

I listened carefully to every word he said. The way he moved and spoke, everything about him, was perfect and magical.

"When you first heard about your destiny, did you not feel like it was a mistake? Did you feel like you were not fit for the task?"

I nodded.

"Why not?"

"Because, I—" I simply didn't have an answer to that question. I stared at him blankly for a moment.

"You didn't believe in yourself, did you?" he asked disappointed. I shook my head, admitting the truth. "The reason why I chose you was not to make your life miserable or make you go through horrible experiences. The reason why I chose you was simply because of how special you are. You have an amazing spirit that I myself admire. Just like these six realms, each and every one of us is a separate world, and we all have spirits in us. That special spirit you have inside of you has guided you throughout your entire journey, and I am proud to say you have done an excellent job listening."

I felt proud of myself when he said that. "What will happen now?" I asked.

"The war is over now, and The Order is safe, thanks to you! Isn't that what you wanted more than anything in the world?" he asked, taking me to my next question. It was like he knew exactly what to ask and what to say. He even knew my doubts.

He just wanted to hear it from me.

"Yes sir, I do." I was trying to find the right words.

"But?" He waited.

"My city was destroyed, and most of the people that fought with me were injured. Some of them even lost their lives. Can you fix it?" I asked, waiting for good news.

"I really wish I could help you, Ethasus, but gods aren't allowed to change history. It may cause the destruction of future destinies."

Destruction of Future Destinies!

I put my head down and stared at the marvel celestial floor in dismay.

I was feeling sad again. I really wanted to help. Yet, he already knew that.

"But don't worry. I'll take good care of them in Paradise," he guaranteed.

I was happy with that answer, and still sad at the same time. I really didn't know what I was feeling really.

He placed his perfect hands on my shoulder, and smiled again.

"Not all is lost," he said. "You've earned yourself a new guardian now."

A new guardian? Who was he talking about? Was it Kate?

"Who?" I asked.

"You'll find out when the time is right."

I gave it a bit of thought. Everything he said made sense now. At least he answered all my questions.

"Thank you for taking a minute of your time and answering my questions, sir. I really appreciate it. I'm honored to have be chosen by you."

I bowed in reverence. Then I looked at Matheus. I was ready to go back to Earth again.

"There is something else, isn't there?" he asked as I turned away.

I looked straight into his eyes and he was concerned. I never expected that. He knew there was something else. Still, I was afraid to ask. I thought it would be very disrespectful to even speak about it. I kept quiet.

"I know you, Ethasus. I know exactly what you want."

I wanted to say it but I just didn't have the guts. I really did feel like a burden.

"I just—I just want to be a normal guy," I finally said.

He smiled again.

"I always knew you did! That's why I gave you an amazing family, awesome friends, and a beautiful girlfriend named Kate!" He winked at me after he said her name.

I felt a little embarrassed, but he was right though. I was as normal as anyone could be! Why ask for more, when I had it all?

"You are absolutely right, sir! I'm such an idiot for even asking that, I apologize," I said feeling stupid and ungrateful.

"You don't have to apologize, Ethasus. All you needed was guidance. You wanted answers, so I opened your eyes, showed you what you needed to see, and told you what you needed to hear."

"Thank you for everything, sir." I bowed again. I had so much respect for him.

"Please, call me Elios," he said kindly.

I couldn't wait to tell everyone back on Earth. I leapt on Matheus' back again. As we descended back to Earth, Elios waved at us. I waved back.

I finally met his excellency, Elios!

EARTH

Two years have passed since the war. New York City is still under construction and people are still searching for answers. They wanted to know who the guardians were? Where was The Book of Mythos? And who was The Chosen One?

Detarru Island is now a place of attraction, tourists, archeology and history.

Thanks to Christine and her connections to some government officials, Erick's identity has been well classified. No one speaks about it, and no one to this day knows who The Chosen One really is.

—ERICK is now 18 years old. Today is June 19th and it is his birthday. Ever since he started school, he fit right in and became one of the popular kids. He also became captain of the football team and everyone loved him. After he saw what a great leader and team captain Erick turned out to be, MIKE and Erick became best of friends. Since then, they've been inseparable.

—JACK became a famous professor at NYU. There he teaches the history of Detarru Island to many of his students, and many who admire his work as an archeologist. He got awarded for his research and now his findings are part of The National Museum of History. One of his favorite college students was BRUCE. There Bruce became Jack's personal assistant and after learning so much about Jack's research, Bruce became fascinated by archeology and respected his work.

—CLARA now owns the GBI Corporation. She funds many charities and smaller businesses who needed support after the war. After graduating from high school, Jimmy got an internship at GBI and there he applied his management skills and helped Clara by overseeing and supervising the business operations. A few months later, the company grew tremendously and is now number one in the world.

—HARRIS and CHRISTINE moved a few blocks away from Sunnyside Street and Erick loves the idea. He visits them every day and goes fishing with his grandparents once in a while. There is nothing he enjoyed more than spending time with his old folks.

—MATT finally retired and bought a house on the beach in Tampa Florida. There he lives happily with his best friend MATHEUS. Occasionally, Matheus will sneak out and come visit Erick once in a while and fly him around the city. Erick helped him develop his transformation skills and little by little he was able to transform into many more things in different dimensions.

—CRAIG decided to work at the Metropolitan Museum of Art. As Erick's new guardian, he wanted to make sure The Gates of Hell were well secured. He also hired trusted Detarrunians to guard all seven gates around the world.

—NATHAN felt really lucky to have REBECCA as a friend and she felt the same way about him too. They fell deeply in love and a year later, he decided to propose. They are going to get married soon and can't wait to tell everyone the news.

—PATRICK joined the military and served in the marines for a year and a half. There he got in shape and is now better looking than the rest of the archangels. He became great friends with

Justin and Chris. Sarah and Chris consider him part of the family and he visits them all the time.

—Luis loves baseball so much he got drafted to the New York Yankees. He became one of the best players on the team and drives the Latinas crazy. Once in a while, he gets front row tickets just to have the guys support and watch him play. Erick and Larry always have a blast cheering for him and whenever he's free, he gathers the rest of the team and they play a game at the stadium just like old times.

—Larry developed a need for speed and soon after graduation, he became a racecar driver. He won many championships and started to get recognized in the sport. A few months later, he got his racing license and is starting to get calls to compete in real NASCAR races.

—Kate pursued her career in medicine and was accepted at one of the best medical universities in New York. Erick and Kate are both madly in love with each other and their relationship strengthens more and more throughout the years.

That night

Sarah invited everyone for dinner to celebrate Erick's 18th birthday. Clara was talking about Jimmy's promotion as a business manager in her company, and Rebecca announced her wedding date for December. Everyone had a wonderful time together celebrating the good news. Hours later, Craig received a distress phone call from one of the security officers at the museum. He was told that The Gates of Hell were activating, and that he needed to come quickly. Everyone thought it was Satu.

Erick and the boys immediately headed to the museum with Craig. When they got there, there were police officers outside and choppers hovering over the building. They all had their guns pointing at something.

Two hollows and a demon.

Erick thought he was dreaming.

He walked up the stairs, but a police officer tried to hold him back.

"It's okay, officer," he said calmly. "They're friendly."

The officer looked at Erick awkwardly but then moved out of his way. Erick slowly walked up to the demon who was standing by the main entrance of the building.

Then he remembered something The Creator, Elios, had told him two years ago.

'You've earned yourself a new guardian now!'

He smiled at her.

"Of course! Guardians don't die!" he exclaimed. He hugged the demon who was now part of his team. His new guardian!

Craig and the boys couldn't believe it either.

"I'm so glad you're alive, Lola!" Erick said, excited.

"I'm glad to see you too, Ethasus!" She smiled. "I'm sorry to barge into your world like this, but we've got trouble," she said with a serious voice.

"Satu?" he asked, concerned

"No. Far worse than that. The angel of death. Abaddon."

Erick turned to his archangels. They were ready to save the world once more.

THE END

Acknowledgments

Nothing is more exciting to me than having an idea and sharing it with the whole world through a book. I couldn't have done it without the help of my great friends, coworkers and family who have been supporting me since day one. Special thanks to my editor Sherrie who helped me make this possible. Her editing was very professional and she was very helpful. You are awesome!

To my book designers Rebecacovers and Albert Nouel, you both are super talented and I'm super happy with my cover. Thank you to Euan Monaghan, who designed the internal pages.To my readers, thank you all, for supporting my work and for believing in me.

About the Author

Mickey Deymon enjoys painting, writing, acting, filming and music. She developed a passion for film after her first project in 2010 in which she directed and acted. Besides her passion for the film industry, she also wrote her first book *Detarru Island* in 2012 and had the opportunity to be published in the year 2018.

"Filming and writing is a gateway to my imagination. It is a place where I can escape reality for a moment in time and forget about my problems in life. It is such a great feeling to have an idea or a memory and share it with the rest of the world either through writing or a motion picture. One that you'll never forget and will always remember. Every time I film, I have the need for more. Every time I write, I feel the need to film. Through writing, I can express my feelings. Through film, I show the world what life is about. Life is a book, every day is a different chapter. Every choice you make creates a different scenario in which you must try to resolve, and based on the decisions that you make, that is how you'll know how your story is going to end. As usual we don't always like certain endings, but that is why today we are still striving and trying to succeed in life. Now that I found my true calling, nothing will stop me now. Welcome to the beginning of my life's expedition: the beginning of story telling through writing or a Motion Picture because that's what makes me happy. That's what makes me stronger and that's where I belong."

www.ingramcontent.com/pod-product-compliance
Lightning Source LLC
Chambersburg PA
CBHW050034180626
46810CB00002B/717